INCIDENT AT BUTLER'S STATION

For Cavalry Sergeant Ed Blaine, wounded by an Apache lance, the way station offered a chance to recover. All he wanted was a place to rest. But it was not to be . . . First he met up with the girl he had once been about to marry. Then he found himself under the guns of a bunch of outlaws waiting to free their brother from an incoming stage. Then, just when Blaine figured it couldn't get any worse, Butler's Station was hit by a band of warring Apaches . . .

NEIL HUNTER

◆

INCIDENT AT BUTLER'S STATION

Complete and Unabridged

LINFORD
Leicester

First published in Great Britain in 1967

First Linford Edition
published 2016

Copyright © 1967, 2005 by Michael R. Linaker

A catalogue record for this book is available
from the British Library.

ISBN 978–1–4448–2824–5

Published by
F. A. Thorpe (Publishing)
Anstey, Leicestershire

Set by Words & Graphics Ltd.
Anstey, Leicestershire
Printed and bound in Great Britain by
T. J. International Ltd., Padstow, Cornwall

This book is printed on acid-free paper

1

The way station lay close to the foothills of the Mohawk Mountains. The land here was still rough and harsh, but somehow managed to support a few skinny trees and sprawling clumps of tough, tangled brush.

A log and adobe cabin, a weather-beaten barn and a split-pole corral made up the station. And a faded, peeling, sign over the cabin door — *BUTLER'S STATION* — made it official. The whole place had a run-down and sun-bleached look about it that fitted in with the surrounding country.

By day the cabin sat beneath the sun's blinding glare, and at night its wooden structure cracked and popped in the chill winds that blew from the vast-reaching desert land which lay over to the south and east.

Fifty yards from the back of the

cabin, through a sprawling mass of tangled brush, ran a narrow creek, winding its way across the hard empty land. For a few yards along its banks grass had managed to grow and stay, adding a touch of color to the otherwise drab and dreary yellow-ochre and gray landscape.

Beyond the creek the land rose in a series of undulations to a low ridge that ran from east to west for a few miles. And beyond the ridge the land began its long slow climb to the peaks of the Mohawk range.

The cabin itself faced south. The land lay practically flat here, and seemed to spread to infinity. This was a rocky, sun-scorched land composed mainly of hard-topped earth, sand and volcanic rock. It was a cruel, lonely, empty land where the only living residents were lizards and snakes. Man came here only when he had to. Even the Apache, who was on home ground, became wary and took no chances when he entered this forsaken land.

Dawn came slowly to this land. The blackness of night paled to a streaky gray. Landmarks took on solid form as the grayness spread across the wide sky. From the rim of the far horizon the first pale fingers of the new day's light crept into view. The stars faded before the advancing fingers of pink flowed into a baleful orange flood that stained the sky with its glow.

The chill dampness of night vaporized in the spreading warmth, filling the ground hollows with a fine milk-white mist. The ground took on the reddening splash thrown out by the sun. The rocks, the brush, the whole earth became a mass of flowing, blood-red color as the dull, pulsing orb kept on its predetermined journey into the heavens.

Full daylight came and the final shadows of night fled.

The land lay open and naked under the searing eye of fire that hung in the cloudless blue of the big sky. Probing fingers of light crept through the cracks in the walls of the cabin at Butler's Station. They entered silently, darting brightly across wooden floors, seeking out the dim corners, filling the cabin with the light of a new day.

★　★　★

Katy Warner had wakened in the first light of dawn. She had rolled on to her side and watched the world come alive through the single tiny window of her small room.

Now, as full, soft shafts of sunlight lanced in at her through the dusty glass, she rolled on to her back and gave a deep sigh. She stared up at the ceiling for a long while.

Finally she threw back the bedclothes and swung her feet to the floor. Standing, she crossed over to the window and gazed out. She could see the water of the creek sparkling in the fresh brightness of the morning. Turning from the window she picked up her clothes from a chair beside the bed.

Silently opening the door, she stepped out of the bedroom and went swiftly down the short corridor into the kitchen. Unlocking the cabin's rear door, she paused long enough to pick up a cake of soap and a towel; then she stepped outside, closing the door behind her.

The warmth of the morning soaked through the thin cotton nightdress she wore as she made her way across the open stretch of ground that lay between the cabin and the creek. Pushing through a gap in the thick brush, Katy came to the bank of the creek. Dropping her bundle on the thin grass at her feet, she gathered the nightdress in her hands, and drew it up her body over her head.

She stood for a moment, enjoying the warm sun on her flesh. She was a tall, firm-bodied woman, small of waist, with full, curving hips and thighs. As she moved her breasts trembled tautly and her long, deep-copper hair tumbled about her shoulders. Bending, she picked up the cake of soap, then stepped into the clear flowing water of the creek.

Katy shivered as the cold water came in contact with her smooth flesh, pale and white except where the sun had caught her face and arms. She ducked under for a moment, rising wet and glistening, her hair hanging in thick ropes.

She began to hum softly as she started to soap herself.

★　★　★

The creak of bedsprings in the next room told Ham Butler that Katy Warner was getting up. He slipped off his own bed and crouched by the window, waiting. A minute or so later he heard the rear door of the cabin open. Then he saw her walking in the direction of the creek in her nightdress, her hips swinging in that loose, graceful way that made his lips go dry and his heart pound.

Sliding open his window, Ham climbed through and ran in a silent crouch, heading for a spot a few yards upstream from where Katy Warner had gone into the brush.

Ham Butler was a long, thin youth of twenty. He wore faded Levis and shirt, scuffed, run-down boots. He was a pale, sickly-looking boy, with deep-set, dark eyes, a narrow nose, a thin, limp mouth. His hair was dark and long, uncombed for some time. Crusted dirt-rings circled his wrists and thin neck.

But for all his gangling appearance, he made no noise as he slid into the thickness of the brush.

He saw her straightaway. She was standing at the edge of the creek. She was naked. Ham felt his face flush, his eyes water as he looked at her. She stood with her back to him, the sunlight rippling across the thick strands of hair.

Then she bent to pick up a cake of soap and he saw the momentary tautness in the muscles of her thighs, saw the barest quiver of her buttocks.

Ham clenched his sweating hands to his sides. A cold smile played on his thin lips as he watched the woman step into the water of the creek.

Now who's laughing? he was asking himself. *Now who's doing the laughing? It's me. Me!* But he felt his eyes sting as he remembered when it was she who was laughing.

Laughing as she slapped his face for trying to kiss her. As she told him to wait a few years before he tried to do a man-size job. He still went hot when he recalled that day.

She'd made him look like a fool. Ham couldn't forget it. So now he would wait for her to come down to the creek and he'd follow, hide and watch. He could see all he wanted, and she knew nothing about it. Stupid bitch! Ham forced back a giggle. What the hell would she do if she found out what he'd been doing? She'd probably blush right down to the ends of her toes.

Serve her right! Bitch!

Ham stiffened as he saw Katy step out of the creek, water spilling from her hips and thighs. He stayed long enough to see her dry herself with a towel, then he wormed his way out of the brush and went silently back to the cabin.

Back in his room he closed the window and waited. Shortly he saw her emerge from the brush. She was dressed now. A faded man's shirt, washed-out Levi's that hugged her hips and legs, emphasizing the flatness of her stomach. The Levi's were pulled over the tops of worn high-heeled riding boots.

The rear door clicked shut as she entered the kitchen.

Ham smiled to himself, stretched out on his bed, and lay staring at the ceiling, waiting for her to call that breakfast was ready.

★   ★   ★

Somewhere, far away, he heard a loud, insistent thumping.

He moved slowly, sluggishly, feeling the bed sway beneath his weight. Like every other morning he came awake slowly. He slept deeply, heavily, never feeling refreshed from it.

The thumping continued. Now he could hear a voice as well. His eyes opened. They felt puffy and they ached. There was a sour stickiness in his mouth, too. Again he heard the voice.

'Chad? You awake? I'm dishing breakfast up in five minutes.'

Chad Butler pushed himself to a sitting position. He ran a hand through his hair, scratching the top of his head. 'Okay, Katy, gimme a minute,' he yelled. His throat was dry and his words came out rasping and thin.

The thumping ceased. He heard Katy go to the door of Ham's room and start to rouse him. After a few seconds he heard Ham's shrill voice.

Chad climbed out of bed. He stretched noisily, blowing air through his nose. He didn't need to dress because he'd gone to bed with his clothes on. Most nights now he did the same. He saw no reason why not. And, anyhow, most nights he was so damn tired he couldn't be bothered to undress. Trouble was that Katy was bound to go on at him about making the bedclothes dirty. He glanced at them.

They did look a mite grubby. *Well, hell*, he thought, *I take my damn boots off, don't I?*

He wondered whether he ought to shave today. There was a cracked mirror on the wall beside his bed. Chad peered into it. He rubbed his hand across his stubbled jaw.

He decided he could leave it another day. *You ugly old bastard*, he muttered mentally as he studied his face in the dust-streaked mirror. His reflection winked back at him, then stared with puffy, bloodshot eyes. His nose twitched as he sniffed loudly.

Turning from the mirror, he sat on the edge of the bed and began to pull on his boots. The effort left him panting for breath, his flabby face red with exertion.

'Damn this god-awful country,' he grumbled out loud. 'Hell, it's only break-fast time and already it's too hot to move.'

He sat for a moment. He swore strongly and forcibly about the land

and the heat and the food and everything in general. He did this every morning. Finally he was forced to stop. The only reason was that there was nothing more he could swear about.

Then he heard Katy Warner shouting from the kitchen.

'All right, I'm comin',' he yelled back. Then in a lower tone, 'Goddamn women. Don't give a man time to get his britches on.'

He gave a harsh chuckle at that. *One thing about going to bed in your clothes*, he thought, *you ain't likely to be caught with your britches down*. Chad thought this real funny. He got off the bed grinning like a school kid. He began to laugh as he opened the door and made for the kitchen. He was thinking that maybe today was going to be a good day.

Maybe an unusually good day. For a change. And while he thought about it, he realized that anything able to break the monotony would make a good day. Christ, anything. Anything at all.

2

About four hours' ride to the north west of Butler's Station, where the land was open and rocky, a weary, dust-caked sorrel mare plodded slowly down a slight dip in the ground. Flies worried the animal constantly, and it used its tail in a vain effort to get rid of them. The insects would disperse for a few seconds, then return.

Some of them, however, decided to try for something else. They chose the mare's rider. He sat his saddle loosely. His hands were clasped around the saddle pommel in an attempt to keep himself on the sorrel's back. His head was tilted forward, his chin against his chest. Like the animal he rode, he was covered with dust. It was fine gray alkali dust that clung to him from head to foot like a second skin. He might have been a figure carved from stone if it hadn't been for the patch of congealed blood that made a vivid stain down the back of his shirt. The snapped-off shaft of an Apache lance jutted from the center of the stain. The lance head was buried deep in the man's right shoulder. Flies began to hover around the wound, and as the man became aware of them he raised his head.

Beneath the brim of his hat his face was in shadow. Sweat had gouged jagged paths through the dust that filmed his face. His lips were raw and cracked. Blood had dried and blackened on them. From deep in their sockets his eyes stared straight ahead . . . seeing, yet unseeing . . . for he was completely exhausted, and despite the heat his body shivered with fever.

As he moved, very slowly and painfully, the hardened layer of dust and sweat cracked and peeled away from his left sleeve. His shirt was dark blue in color, and on his sleeve he wore the stripes and diamond of a U.S. Cavalry sergeant.

The slow-footed sorrel stumbled, jolting its rider. The man felt white-hot streaks of pain in his back. A low sound passed his lips. His hands clenched hard on the pommel, the knuckles showing white against the brown of the rest of his hand.

Regaining its balance the sorrel plodded on. The land lay wide and flat and empty around horse and rider. And above them the sky too was empty, save for the yellow disc of fire that burned relentlessly, cruelly, regardless of what went on below.

★   ★   ★

Four men rode towards Butler's Station that morning.

Four men with thoughts of murder on their minds.

They were brothers. The Reece brothers. Matthew the eldest. Then Jubal and Ned. And Hoby, youngest of them all, but at twenty-one, a ruthless, brutal killer like the rest of the clan.

15

They were silent as they rode. Each man cloaked in his own thoughts, each keeping his attention, his concentration on what lay head.

The previous night they had bedded down in a dry wash. After a cold meal each man had rolled up in his blanket and rested. At dawn they had again eaten a swift cold meal. Then they had saddled up and moved out at a slow pace.

They didn't hurry. They didn't need to. They knew where they were going and how long it would take to get there.

Matthew Reece raised an arm and reined in his mount. His brothers halted their own horses and waited for him to speak.

Saddle leather creaked as Matthew Reece shifted his weight. He was a big man, broad across the shoulders and chest. Beneath the brim of his hat his face was wide, the flesh laid over big bones. His eyes were black and bright like a bird's. He hadn't shaved for four or five days and the stubble was thick and dark across his jaw. From his shirt pocket he took out a gold-cased watch. Opening the cover he glanced at the face. He then carefully closed the cover after giving a satisfied nod, and replaced the watch in his pocket.

'What's it say, Matt?' Jubal asked slowly. He was two years younger than Matthew. A large awkward man, heavy on his feet, he moved with a ponderous motion that belied his tremendous strength. He was a dull-witted man, too, slow to understand things, though easily aroused to frightening and uncontrollable violence. He alone of the Reeces had no weapon strapped around his waist or jammed into the saddle boot.

'It's ten minutes past nine,' Matthew said. He spoke slowly, pronouncing his words clearly and audibly. Jubal listened, then nodded, satisfied.

'You sure that thing's right? Hoby asked irritably.

'This watch ain't had a wrong minute ever,' Matthew said. 'It did right for Pa nigh on twenty-five years. I reckon it'll do for us.'

'Don't pay him no attention, Matt,'

Ned Reece said. He held his hat in his hand while he wiped his face with a soiled bandanna. 'You reckon we'll be there on time?'

'We will,' Matthew assured him.

Jubal looked across at Matthew. His face bore a strained expression and his lips moved laboriously.

'We got to be there on time,' he said slowly. 'We got to be there for Sid. We got to be.'

Matthew Reece nodded. He raised a big hand to rub his sweating face.

'For Sid,' he repeated.

★　★　★

Far to the east of Butler's Station the land was at its hardest.

Barren and rocky, semi-arid desert, it gave no chance to anything that tried to grow. Here the dust of ages had settled and carpeted the earth with a deep layer. Most of the time the dust lay undisturbed, unmoved for long stretches of time; but sometimes it was agitated

18

and would rise and hover in the hot air for hours, long after the cause of its disturbance had gone.

The heavy, lumbering Concord coach, with its six-horse team, raised a great deal as it rattled its noisy way westward.

The driver and guard, sitting high on the box, were practically free from the clouds of choking, foul-tasting mist. However, inside the coach the passengers were not so lucky.

Dust came swirling through the windows and even seeped up through the floorboards. Added to the constant jerking and swaying of the coach body and the cloying heat, the occupants weren't exactly having a pleasurable trip.

Not that they were complaining. Even if conditions had been perfect, the journey would still have been somewhat grim.

Three of the four passengers were lawmen. A U.S. Marshal and, under him, two deputies.

The fourth passenger was a convicted outlaw on his way to start a long term in Yuma prison.

The prisoner's hands and feet were shackled.

United States Marshal Frank McAllister watched his prisoner carefully. This was to be his last job. When he handed in his prisoner he also handed in his badge.

Thirty years, wasn't it? Pity it was over. *Ah, well, got to make room for the young ones,* he thought. Anyhow, come a few weeks he'd be joining his daughter Lou and her husband Phil at their ranch out near Bisbee. And there'd be little Frank, his grandson. He suddenly had the notion that maybe retirement wouldn't be so bad after all. One thing he regretted was that Mary wasn't living any more. She'd been dead all of five years now.

Seemed a shame. A wife goes through all the hard times with a man, then when the good days come she isn't there to enjoy them with him.

The coach gave a jolt. Beside McAllister sat Harvy Martin. He was a young, eager kid. This was his first major assignment as a deputy marshal and he was bursting with importance, hoping to have some crisis occur so that he could show off his paces. McAllister saw himself as he was thirty years ago every time he looked at Martin.

Martin's hat had come off when the coach jolted. He leaned forward to pick it up from the floorboards.

McAllister's second deputy, Tom Peak, an experienced lawman, sat beside the prisoner on the opposite seat. Peak cradled a shotgun in his arms. As he saw Martin bend forward to pick up his hat, Peak swung the shotgun round.

Then he dropped the barrels to the level of Martin's eye.

'Leave it be,' he said.

Martin straightened up, his face flushed.

'Hey, Tom, what you playin' at?'

Peak used the shotgun to hook Martin's hat. He raised it and Martin took it and shoved it on the back of his head.

'You do that too often and one day your prisoner will reach out and take your gun and use it to blow the top off your head.'

Martin glanced down at his holstered Colt, then across at the prisoner's hands. The expression on his face showed he realized how near he had come to being shot with his own gun.

'*Ouch!* I guess I got a lot to learn,' he said.

'Don't worry, Harv,' McAllister said. 'Ain't no shame in having to be told these things. Better than learnin' the hard way.'

'Listen to the General, kid,' the prisoner said. He was smiling. 'He'll keep you on the right trail.'

'You won't be so cheerful when you hear the gate shut behind you at Yuma,' Peak said.

The prisoner was still smiling when he said, 'You ain't got me there yet, lawman.' He spoke *lawman* like it was a dirty word.

He leaned back in his seat, smiling like a man without a trouble in the world.

His name was Sid Reece.

3

With breakfast over, the routine work at Butler's Station was tackled.

Katy Warner busied herself cleaning up the cabin and preparing the midday meal.

Out in the barn Chad Butler began checking over the stock. He'd received a letter, delivered by one of the outward-bound coaches, that had informed him of a special coach, which would be passing through on the fourth of the month. That was today. *Have to be ready*, Chad reminded himself. *Never know who's going to step off a special. Hell, it might even be the area superintendent come to have a look round. Better give the animals a good brushing down. Make 'em shine.*

Chad looked round for Ham. The boy was nowhere in sight. Chad was about to call him, but changed his mind. It was no good. He couldn't do a damn thing with the kid.

Ham, he decided, was lazy. Pure damn lazy. Chad said the hell with it and chose to do the job himself. If he did put Ham to doing it, the boy would grumble and slouch about, make a mess of it. *It'll get done faster if I do it myself*, he reckoned.

He'd been working for half an hour when he heard the distant sound of a handgun being fired. Two more shots followed. Chad wiped his sweating face and straightened up. *Christ, I'm getting past this*, he thought.

Chad knew now where Ham was. He swore. Ever since the boy had got hold of that old Colt, he spent hours practicing with it. Gun-crazy, Chad called him. Damn head's so full of wild ideas about being a fast-gun he don't give a hoot about anything else. Anger rose briefly but Chad forced it back. The hell with him! He turned back to the horses and spent his anger in a burst of energy. He felt sweat pouring down his back. His shirt was wet with it and clung to his body in clammy folds.

Ham stood with his legs apart, his right hand hovering over the butt of the .45 caliber Colt that lay in the low-cut holster. A rawhide thong held the holster tight against his thigh.

He'd set up a row of empty bottles and cans on the edge of the creek. It had taken three shots to hit the first bottle.

Ham wiped his moist palm across the front of his dirty shirt. He directed his attention to the second bottle. His body swayed slightly as he tried to relax. Ham took a couple of deep, slow breaths.

Suddenly his right hand dropped to the worn butt of the Colt. As his fingers curled around the butt his thumb was in line with the hammer. The gun slid free of the oiled leather, rose up and forward. Ham felt the hammer click back. Then the muzzle leveled and Ham tripped the trigger. He felt the Colt slap back against his palm, heard the deep roar as the barrel spat out a tongue of flame.

The bottle exploded in a burst of shattered glass.

Ham grinned proudly. *That's more like it*, he thought.

Returning the Colt to its holster, Ham rubbed his hand across his shirt again.

He dipped his hand again. It rose in a blur, and the Colt roared once again. Elation swept through Ham as he saw one of the cans kick away and go flying across the creek.

Spinning the Colt on his finger, Ham swaggered over to the creek bank and sprawled on the thin layer of grass. He pulled a ragged cloth from his pants and cleaned the Colt carefully and thoroughly. When he'd finished, he removed the belt and holster and lay the gear down beside him.

Ham lay back, feeling the sun warm on him. He closed his eyes and listened to the murmur of the creek against the bank.

The morning was almost over by the time Katy Warner got through her work. With the cabin sorted out and the midday meal on the stove she had time to brew a pot of coffee. Filling a large mug, she went out the back door and headed for the barn.

Chad glanced up from his work as she came into the barn. He put down his brushes and stepped out of the stall. His face was shiny with sweat, his shirt dark and wet.

'Bless you, Katy,' he said.

'You sure do look busy,' she said as she handed him the coffee.

Chad took a mouthful of the hot black coffee. He grinned, wiping his face on his shirt sleeve.

'Ain't gonna have no smart-aleck company man catching me out,' he said between swift gulps of coffee.

'Well, the cabin's shining like a copper kettle,' Katy told him. She gazed round the barn. 'Where's Ham?' she demanded.

'Ah, he's off somewhere with that damn gun of his,' Chad mumbled.

Katy shook her head angrily. 'Chad, you're too soft with him. Gracious, he's old enough to do his share.'

Chad scratched his head. He handed the empty mug back to Katy. 'Yeah, I know,' he said. 'Thanks for the coffee, Katy. I better get on.'

He turned back into the stall.

'I'm getting lunch,' Katy called. 'I'll give you a yell when it's ready.'

'Yeah, okay,' Chad replied over his shoulder.

Katy turned and stepped out of the comparative coolness of the barn and into the blinding glare of the midday sun. She began to stride across the yard, moving towards the cabin. For no reason at all she suddenly glanced up.

She stopped dead in her tracks. Directly across her path stood a dust-caked horse. The animal's head was low, its sides rippled and shuddered as it turned to look at her with weary, almost pleading eyes.

But Katy had all her attention focused on the horse's rider. A man who held himself in the saddle by clinging to the pommel. As her eyes took in the dust-caked clothes, she saw the length of the lance that jutted from the man's back.

The mug she was holding dropped from her fingers as the sun-blistered, blood-streaked face of the man turned toward her. Deep inside her she felt something stir as she saw the face. His lips moved. Silently. Then she said one word. '*Ed!*' She spoke it in a shocked, breathless whisper.

The man stiffened at the sound of her voice. The horse moved restlessly. A low groan came from the cracked lips as the man's head fell forward on to his chest. He leaned in the saddle, then keeled over and toppled to the ground.

He lay on his face. Fresh, bright blood welled out of the wound around the lance-head.

Katy, her face very pale, took one hesitant step forward.

Then she turned toward the barn.

'*Chad!*' she yelled at the top of her voice.

As the clear, sharp note of her voice cut the air the horse's ears pricked up and its eyes rolled. It gave a nervous snort. But it was too exhausted to do any more than that.

4

Between them they managed to carry the unconscious man into the cabin. Chad's face was red with the effort as he and Katy lowered their burden on to the heavy kitchen table.

'If some of the people who've eaten off this here table knew some of the things it's been used for,' Chad remarked. He gave a low chuckle as he thought about it.

Katy filled a big kettle and put it on the stove. Then she fed a few hunks of wood into the flames and gave it a poke.

'See if you can find those strips of white rag I told you about,' Chad said.

While Katy was looking for the rags, Chad gave his hands a good scrub. Then from the kitchen cupboard he took a narrow, cloth-wrapped bundle. From the cloth he drew two thin-bladed knives, sharpened to an extremely keen edge.

Katy came back with the bundle of rags and Chad took them from her.

'There's a bottle of surgical spirit in the cupboard, Katy,' he told her. 'Get it out and give these knives a good dosing.'

As Katy sterilized the knives, Chad shuffled off to his bedroom. He returned a couple of minutes later, wearing an ankle-length white cotton coat. The front of the coat was blotchy with faded rust-colored stains.

'Hell, I done so much of this thing I feel like a real damn doctor in this rig,' he said.

Moving to the table he checked the man's pulse. Nodding with satisfaction, he took one of the knives and slit open the blood-soaked shirt. Then he leaned forward to inspect the wound.

'He was lucky. Shoulder muscle took it. Stopped it going in deep. Should get it out without too much fuss. He's a big one, ain't he?' he said. Chad spoke as if he were discussing a side of beef. He glanced across at Katy. 'You sure you want to stay? Might get a little messy.'

She nodded. 'I'll be all right. I've seen worse things than this,' she said soberly, though there was a faint tremor in her voice.

Nodding, Chad said, 'See if that water's ready.'

Katy moved swiftly, filling a basin with the boiling water and placing it in a handy position for Chad.

Soaking a piece of rag Chad began the slow, careful job of cleaning away the hard, congealed blood from around the wound. It took a long time. Katy refilled the basin with fresh water three times before Chad finished.

Finally wiping his bloody hands down the front of his coat he said, 'Now the trouble starts.'

He took the bottle of spirit and poured some on to a clean rag. Then he wiped around the wound with it, letting some of the clear liquid run into the torn flesh. The man on the table gave a sudden groan and moved. Katy glanced up at Chad. He was picking up one of the knives. 'Lean on his shoulders. Try and keep him still for a few seconds.'

She nodded and positioned herself.

'Okay?' Chad asked.

Katy nodded. But her stomach was doing things it was not supposed to.

She watched, almost fascinated, as the knife did its swift work. A harsh, bubbling groan came from the man's lips. Katy felt him twist and jerk against her restraining hands.

The struggles lasted for only brief seconds. Then they ceased. Katy felt a warm wetness on her hands. Bright blood had spurted from the wound, streaking her fingers and wrists.

'Now hold him again. Real hard this time,' Chad said. 'When I give you a nod, hang on.'

He placed one hand firmly on the naked back. With the other he grasped hold of the lance-shaft as close to the wound as possible. Katy saw him take a deep breath. Then she saw his nod. Katy pressed down hard. She saw Chad clench his teeth, heard him grunt.

For a moment nothing happened. Katy felt the man on the table quiver. A few seconds passed. Then the head of the lance moved slightly. Chad's face shone with sweat. He blinked his eyes to clear them. The man on the table gave a low groan. Katy felt her heart pounding against her ribs.

'Move, damn you, move, move,' Chad mumbled darkly, and despite the tension Katy gave a quick smile.

Abruptly the lance-head came free. Chad gave an explosive gasp. There was a sudden spurt of hot red blood from the gaping hole. Katy clenched her teeth as she felt it splash on to the front of her shirt and Levi's.

A tortured moan came from the man. His body quivered, then thrust up against Katy's hands. For a moment she felt panic rising in her. But Chad was beside her, gripping the writhing figure with his strong hands. He held on until the convulsions ceased and the man lay still again.

'Okay, let's get this bleeding stopped.

Then we can get him all tied up and bandaged. I reckon he'll be all right.'

He grinned. 'These cavalry fellers are sure tough characters, huh?'

He fell silent for a while. Then he said, 'Sergeant, eh? Wonder what his name is.'

'Edwin Blaine,' Katy said softly.

'*Huh?*' Chad glanced up, puzzled.

'His name. Edwin Blaine,' Katy repeated.

'You know him?'

Katy nodded. She was far away in thoughts and memories. In another place at another time.

'You know him well?' Chad asked, persisting with his questions now that he was on to something.

Katy smiled at that. She glanced up at Chad. Her eyes were moist with tears.

'We were going to be married,' she told him.

5

It was twelve o'clock straight up by Frank McAllister's watch when the swaying coach began to slow down. It finally came to a creaking halt. McAllister poked his head out of the side window.

'Hey, Sam, you nearly didn't make it,' he called.

Sam Loren, the driver, leaned over the edge of his seat. His leathery brown face, almost hidden by a black beard, split into a craggy, lined grin. 'Bet you a goddamn month's pay it's noon. On the dot,' he said.

McCallister opened his door and climbed stiffly to the ground. 'Sure am glad I'm not a gambling man,' he said.

Sam Loren got down off his box and McCallister asked, 'How long we going to stop here, Sam?'

Loren scratched his bearded chin.

'No more'n an hour. I want to give the team a rest before they start the pull up to Butler's Station. Country starts to get high round here. We're gettin' near the Mohawks.'

'We could do with a rest,' McAllister said. He blinked his aching eyes, licked his dry lips, wishing he could get away from the dust and heat. Christ, though, he was feeling stiff. Hurting every place. *It's sure time you retired*, he told himself.

Turning, he raised a hand to Tom Peak. 'All right, fetch him out. Get some fresh air and some exercise. We'll be here for about an hour.'

Inside the coach Peak made a short movement with his shotgun.

'Go ahead, Reece,' he said. 'Outside. You make one wrong move and I'll let you have both barrels.'

Sid Reece chuckled. He raised his manacled wrists, saying, 'What kind of move could I make with this lot on me?'

'Just a warning, that's all,' Peak said evenly.

'Yeah.'

Reece pushed himself awkwardly out of the coach. He moved slowly and clumsily because the shackles round his ankles were fastened by a short chain. He leaned against the side of the coach and stared out over the vast spread of land that stretched into the far distance, finally becoming lost in the glare of the sun. He was a tall man, strongly built. His face was brown and hard, his eyes black and swift and cold.

Harvy Martin climbed down from the coach and paused beside Reece. He followed Reece's gaze, then grinned. 'If you're looking for them brothers of yours, forget it. They ain't goin' to bother coming for you. Why, we'd finish off a bunch of no-good scum like them in a . . .'

Martin's words were choked off in a gasp of pain as Sid Reece spun round and smashed his shackled fists into his face. Martin bounced off the side of the coach, blood streaking the side of his face. He gave a grunt, and stepped forward. His young looks had Sid Reece fooled. Martin's right fist crashed against Reece's forehead. Another slammed into the outlaw's stomach. As Reece sagged forward, Martin swung his right again in a smashing, tearing blow that caught Reece full on the mouth. The sound of the punch was loud in the still, clear air. Sid Reece fell hard and lay still.

'Harv, cut that out,' McAllister yelled. He had spun round at the sound of the scuffle.

Peak was out of the coach now. He looked down at Reece, then at Martin. He grinned. 'You okay?'

Martin nodded. He took a kerchief out of his pants and began to wipe blood off his cheek. The chain of Reece's shackles had opened a two-inch gash.

McAllister and Sam Loren pulled Sid Reece to his feet. The outlaw's face was dark with anger, his eyes narrowed. Both his lips were split and blood streaked his chin.

'I want no more of this,' McAllister said harshly. 'If nobody's got anything important to say, then they'd better keep quiet. You listening, Harv?'

Martin nodded. 'I hear.'

Reece gave a short laugh. 'Hear me, too, boy. This ain't finished yet. I promise.'

'Shut it, Reece,' McAllister snapped. 'Mister, you just watch out or you'll find I ain't as old and soft as I look.'

Reece leaned against the side of the coach. He fell silent, his face still as he wiped at the blood on his chin.

The duration of the halt passed in an uncomfortable silence. Each man gave an inner sigh of relief when Sam Loren climbed up on his seat and said, 'All set, Frank.'

'Okay, Sam. Everybody inside. Let's go.'

While his deputies got the prisoner on board, McAllister walked around to the guard's side of the coach.

'Will, I want you to keep your eyes open real hard from here on.'

The guard, Will Hakin, nodded. 'Sure thing, Marshal. Anything particular you want me to watch for?'

McCallister shook his head. 'No. Just be on the lookout for anything that looks suspicious.'

'You thinking maybe Reece's brothers might try to take him away from us?' Sam Loren asked.

'It's possible,' McCallister replied. 'Maybe. I'm just fidgeting. Anyhow, it don't hurt to be cautious.'

He turned and climbed into the coach. Up on the box Sam Loren gave the reins a whack and let rip with a loud whoop. The team strained against the leather. The coach gave a drunken lurch, jerked wildly, then began to roll.

* * *

Ham wasn't sure what it was that woke him. He lay for a moment, feeling the sun warm on his body, hearing the sound of the creek. Idly he wondered how long he'd lain here. Then he brushed the thought aside. *Who the hell cares? I ain't bothered what they think. Damn 'em to hell!*

Then he heard the clear, recognizable sound of a horse snorting. It sounded very close. Ham could hear other things now. The jingle of harness and the creak of leather.

Ham opened his eyes and sat up quickly.

Four mounted men formed a tight group in front of him. Men and horses looked tired. Dust coated them thickly. The way the men looked at him made Ham's stomach jerk with fear. They were all hard-faced, cold-eyed men, brothers, too, Ham guessed by their looks.

He remembered his Colt. The gun lay close by. Ham let his right hand slide across the grass. His fingers touched the butt.

'Go ahead, kid, and I'll blow your stupid head open!'

Ham jerked his hand away from the gun. He glanced at the one who'd spoken. The man was young, in fact, not much older than Ham. But for all that, he looked older, much more mature than Ham. His hand hovered over the butt of a low-worn Colt. He looked ready to use it.

'Boy, what's your name?' one of the others asked. He was a big man, strong in body and voice.

'Ham Butler.'

'Your pa run the station yonder?'

Ham nodded. He wondered, *What do they want? Christ, they look like a rough bunch.*

'Anybody else?' asked the big man.

'We got a woman helps out. Name of Katy Warner.'

The young one laughed. 'She young, kid?' and when Ham nodded, 'Pretty?'

'I guess,' Ham muttered.

'Hey, it sounds promising. How you makin' out with her? Laid her yet?'

Ham felt his face redden. He couldn't hold it back. *Bastards*, he spat at them silently. *Dirty bastards.*

'Aw, he's blushing,' the young one said. He tipped back his head and howled with laughter. Even the big man smiled. The other two men were slower to react. One was the biggest man Ham had ever seen. He looked a little stupid to Ham, too. He had a bland, childish grin on his brutish face.

The young man leaned across to this one and gave him a slap across the shoulder.

'Hey, Jubal, looks like there's a feller who's even more scared of girls than you.'

Jubal Reece kept right on grinning. His brow puckered as he digested his brother's words. Then he nodded his great head slowly. His lips moved loosely, then he began to laugh. It was a loud, coarse sound.

To Ham it was a taunting, humiliating sound that beat savagely at his ears. He looked up at the grinning faces of the Reece brothers, wishing he was a million miles from here. These men, strangers, had no right to come here and make fun of him. Especially the one called Jubal. *God*, Ham thought, *I'll bet he's so stupid, he wouldn't know what to do with a woman if'n you put a naked one on a bed for him.*

'Shut your mouth, you stupid bastard!' Ham screamed.

Then instantly wished he'd kept his mouth closed.

Jubal stopped laughing and stared down at Ham.

Like most men of his type, Jubal was an easy target for the crude jokes and insults thrown at him by so-called smart men who seemed to find it highly amusing to torment a fellow creature not so well endowed with the gifts of sharp senses or intelligence. But over a period of time Jubal had caught on to these things. Now he could recognize most of the words that were so often hurled at him in abuse. And he reacted strongly.

Jubal hated being called dumb and crazy and stupid.

Saddle leather creaked as Jubal swung his huge body to the ground. Three strides took him to where Ham Butler crouched.

'I . . . I didn't mean any . . . ' Ham began. Then he gave a whimper of fear. He rolled and grabbed for the Colt. He jerked it from the holster and tried to bring it round to bear on Jubal Reece. Pain lanced up his arm as Jubal's massive fist closed over his wrist. The gun dropped from Ham's fingers.

'Teach him some manners, Jubal,' Matthew Reece said. 'We'll go on ahead to the station. Bring him along when you're through.'

Jubal yanked Ham to his feet, then slammed his huge fist deep into the boy's stomach. Ham screamed as pain filled his body. He could barely breathe. Then Jubal's open palm struck Ham across the face. Ham's head snapped to one side. The hand struck him again and again. He could feel blood in his mouth, feel it rush from his nose. Pain screamed in his stomach again as something hard began to pound there. Bright lights seemed to flash before Ham's eyes. He knew he was scream-ing, begging for it to stop, but he couldn't hear anything.

Then, abruptly, Ham felt his senses fading, and he drifted into unconsciousness. A deep blackness enveloped him, closing out sight and sound and hearing. For a fraction of a second Ham found himself wondering if this was what death was like.

6

Chad held back his questions until they had Ed Blaine settled in one of the small bedrooms at the back of the cabin. Leaving Katy to get Blaine covered, Chad went outside and led the weary sorrel into the barn. He stripped off its saddle and trappings, then gave it a rubdown. He put down feed and fresh water.

When he got back to the cabin, Katy was cleaning up in the kitchen. She glanced up briefly as he came in. 'He's sleeping,' she said.

'Best thing for him just now,' Chad replied. 'Any coffee going?'

'Yes, it's almost ready.' She prepared him a cup as he washed his hands.

Chad took the cup and looked at her for a long silent minute. Then he leaned against the kitchen table.

'Tell me to mind my own business if

you want,' Chad said. 'But what happened?'

Katy stared out of the window. She shrugged her shoulders.

'It was when Ed was at Fort Kane. I worked in a saloon in the settlement near the fort. I met Ed in the saloon. He came in whenever he could. We liked each other. We . . . we fell in love. Ed finally asked me to marry him. I said yes. That was when the trouble started. It seemed the rest of the fort, the women in particular, didn't approve of an intelligent, promotion-due soldier marrying a saloon-girl, a woman who drank and ran around with any kind of man . . . ' She broke off for a time. Then she said, 'One night Ed took me to a dance at the fort. He got into a fight because of something he heard somebody say. He got into trouble over it. And lost his promotion. After that I began to realize that as long as Ed had anything to do with me he was jeopardizing his career. He loves the army. It's his whole life. It would have been selfish of me to go on and marry him. It would have made both our lives miserable. I told Ed, but he said I was being silly. He told me he was going out on a week's patrol and that we'd be married when he returned.'

'And when he came back you'd gone,' Chad finished.

'Yes. I took a stage out and moved around until my money ran out. I hoped he might forget me in time.'

'And when your money ran out, you landed here,' Chad said.

Katy gave a smile. 'Here,' she said. 'I thought this would be an ideal place to stop off at for a while.'

'Seems like he still found you, though he don't know it yet. You plan on running again?'

She was silent then.

'No,' she said. 'I'm not strong enough to do it again.'

'Now you're talking sense,' Chad grinned. 'Now go and get yourself cleaned up.'

Katy glanced down at her blood-stained clothes and hands. She moved to the sink and washed the blood off her hands. As she dried them, she suddenly raised her head and listened intently. She glanced through the window.

'I thought I heard horses,' she said.

Chad joined her.

From the tangled brush that lined the edge of the creek came three riders. They rode slowly, angling toward the cabin. As they got close, one of them broke free from the tight group and reined in near the back door. The other two rode round the side of the cabin.

'Now I wonder what these gents want?' Chad said. 'I get the feeling it isn't exactly a friendly visit. I might be wrong.'

Katy watched the man outside. He dismounted slowly, removing a rifle from his saddle boot. Then he walked toward the kitchen door.

From the front of the cabin came a loud thumping.

Katy glanced at Chad. He shook his head slowly.

'You stay here and watch the feller

outside. I'll go see what our visitors want.' He turned and went out of the kitchen.

The man out back had reached the door now. He opened it and stepped inside, closing and locking the door. He gave a swift look round the kitchen. His eyes finally rested on Katy.

'Ma'am,' he said.

Katy saw a tall, lean man in his late twenties. He would, she thought, be good-looking if he cut his thick hair and had a wash and shave.

The man motioned with his rifle. 'Through there, ma'am,' he said. 'After your friend. Go ahead.'

As Chad crossed the cabin's living room he shrugged out of his bloody smock, draping it across a chair. Reaching the door, he hesitated momentarily. He began to wonder who these men were. What they wanted. Then he heard the kitchen door bang shut, heard the sound of a man's voice.

Chad remembered Katy. And the man with the rifle. He opened the door.

A gun muzzle was pushed into his stomach. The owner of the gun was a slim, grinning youngster of about Ham's age. Behind the young one was an older man. A big man, tough-looking, ruthless even, Chad reckoned, as he looked at Matthew Reece.

'Inside, pop,' Hoby Reece said softly. He prodded Chad's stomach with the muzzle of his long-barrel Colt.

Chad backed up. He didn't say anything. He'd lived long enough to know that in a situation like this it was advisable to play dumb.

Matthew Reece closed the door.

At that moment Katy Warner came in from the kitchen with Ned Reece behind her.

'Hey, hey, this must be the little lady that kid told us about,' Hoby grinned. 'Not bad, huh, Matt?'

Matthew Reece raked his eyes up and down Katy's body. 'Quite a handsome filly,' he said.

'Ain't bad from the rear either,' Ned remarked.

Katy felt color rise the entire length of her face. Anger rose too, and she suddenly whirled around to face Ned Reece. Her right arm swung up and round. Her open palm smacked Ned's face with a loud crack.

Ned Reece took a startled step backward. His jaw dropped open. For a moment it seemed as if he were going to strike her back. But instead he grinned, then laughed. Hoby was laughing too. Matthew Reece stood where he was, smiling coldly. He waited until his brothers quieted down.

'All right, enough horseplay. Hoby, you see to our horses. Then check outside and in the barn. Keep a lookout for any weapons that might be lying about. You check the rest of the cabin, Ned.'

Matthew waited until his brothers had gone about their appointed tasks. He drew his gun.

'This is loaded,' he said, 'and I'll use it if you give me reason. Now both of you sit down.' When Katy and Chad were seated, he said, 'I won't waste time. My name is Matthew Reece. My brothers are Hoby and Ned. There's another, Jubal, you'll meet him later. You've probably heard of us.'

'Who hasn't?' Chad said. 'You're just about the lowest forms of life in the territory.' He spoke as though he had something foul-tasting in his mouth.

Matthew Reece's face hardened visibly. His nostrils flared as he stared angrily at Chad. Then he gave a short laugh. 'Your own words, mister. You know the score then. I won't have to keep telling you just how rough we can make things during our stay.'

'And how long will that be for?' Katy asked acidly.

Matthew glanced at her, his eyes narrowing. 'Don't push your luck too far. I hit ladies just as easy and as hard as men. To answer the question . . . it depends on how long it takes us to carry out a certain job.'

'That being?' Katy questioned.

Matthew turned back to Chad.

'You're expecting a special coach to make a stop here, later today?' Chad nodded. 'There's a man on that coach. He's being taken through to the Yuma pen.'

'Sid Reece,' Chad said suddenly. 'I heard about him.'

Only now did Chad remember the newspaper reports he'd read about Sid Reece's capture and trial.

'That's right. Our brother Sid. Me and the boys don't intend lettin' the law get him to Yuma. We're going to take Sid off that coach when it stops here.' He leaned forward and pointed a finger at Chad. 'And you, Mr. Butler, are going to help us.'

7

Chad Butler didn't show any surprise at Matthew Reece's statement. For a moment he sat quite still. Then he calmly said, 'Sid Reece got what he deserved. He belongs in jail. And I ain't helping to get him free.'

A momentary hardness filmed Matthew Reece's eyes. With startling suddenness his left hand swept up. The back of it slashed across Chad's face. It was a hard, brutal blow. Chad's head fell back with a jerk.

'Don't try to be smart, friend,' Matthew snapped viciously. 'I can keep hitting longer than you can stand it.'

'You . . . animal!' Katy burst out. She was shocked by the deliberate ruthlessness that dominated every move these men made.

Matthew spun round to face her.

'I told you to keep your mouth shut,

lady. Maybe you need a little persua-
din'.' His arm began to rise.

From the rear of the cabin came a
shout. Moments later Ned Reece
appeared in the curtained doorway that
led to the back. Matthew glanced at
him, irritated by the interruption.

'What the hell's up with you?'

'Come and see who's back here,
Matt.'

Katy glanced worriedly at Chad. He
gave her a quick smile. There was a
bruise forming on his right cheek.

'I thought there were only three of
you here,' Matthew spat at Chad.

Chad shrugged. 'There were. Until
today. Now there's four.'

Matthew grunted in anger. He waved
his gun at Katy. She rose and followed
Ned through the curtain. Before Matthew
could follow the cabin door swung open
and Jubal came in. He was dragging the
limp figure of Ham Butler. Chad saw
his son and crossed to him as Jubal let
the boy fall to the floor.

'Keep your eyes on him, Jubal,'

Matthew instructed.

He made his way through to the rear of the cabin, to the room where Ned and Katy waited. Ned pushed open the door and Matthew went in. He bent over the figure in the bed. There was a tight smile on his face when he straightened up.

'By God,' he said, 'this gets better every minute. I was reckoning on it taking a hell of a time to run into this feller Blaine.'

'It'll sure please Sid,' Ned chuckled.

Matthew caught sight of Katy. She was listening closely. 'The lady sure is interested, Ned. You reckon we should tell her about the soldier?'

'Why not? She's gonna find out sooner or later.'

'See, ma'am, Blaine is the feller who caught Sid. Was at Sid's trial too. He don't know us . . . yet . . . but he sure is going to.'

'What are you going to do?' Katy blurted out the question before she could check herself.

It brought a chuckle from Ned. Matthew looked down at the man on the bed.

'We're going to pay him for what he done to Sid, ma'am,' he said.

And the way he said it made Katy's flesh grow cold and clammy despite the heat of the day.

★　★　★

Sam Loren let the team make its own pace now. By his reckoning they would be at Chad Butler's station in about three hours. Be nice to see Chad again, Loren mused, his eyes narrowing as dust swirled up suddenly.

Beside him the guard, Will Hakin, said, 'That feller Reece is a mean one, ain't he, Sam?'

Loren chuckled through his beard. 'He didn't look so mean when that boy dropped him. Ah, hell, Will, them sort are tough and mean when they got a gun in their fist. Take it away and they don't look no different to anybody else.'

The coach lurched without warning, the springs creaked loudly as the wheels hit a rocky stretch of ground.

Sam Loren grabbed for his hat with one hand, holding the plunging lines with the other. A wild, defiant yell broke from his lips as the coach dipped and bucked beneath him.

★ ★ ★

McAllister was feeling it now.

He leaned hard back in his seat, trying to ignore the gnawing, creeping ache that was hammering deep inside him. No matter which way he sat it continued to bite at him. He kept his face blank, his mouth shut tight, though the urge to utter some sound was greater than he'd ever imagined. But he couldn't show it. No matter how he felt.

He was supposed to be in command here. Therefore, he could not show any signs of weakness . . . not in front of his own men. And especially not in front of the prisoner.

Damn it, man, he told himself, *get hold. It's only a touch of old age. God, you've been through worse than this and come out on top.* Then he soberly reflected that those other times had been long ago. And he'd been a hell of a lot younger.

Sid Reece was huddled in the corner of his seat, his head down on his chest. His eyes were closed. He seemed to be asleep. He was, in fact, fully awake. Since the coach had moved off after the halt, he'd been like this.

His face still hurt from Harvy Martin's fists. *All right, you young bastard, I can wait. But watch out when I get these damn chains off. Just see who eats dirt then.*

Sid cursed under his breath as the coach gave another drunken lurch. Dust clouded inside, sifting into his clothes and layering his skin. *Christ, I'll be damn glad when we hit Butler's Station*, he thought. *I sure hope the boys are there. Hell, they'd better be. They've got to be there.* The station was the only sure place to pull off an escape. Out here, on this wide and naked land it was too risky a proposition, too many things could go wrong. But Matt had planned it with his usual care for detail and his calm ruthlessness. Why, he'd even gotten a letter into Sid's cell, back in the town where they were holding him prior to his transportation to Yuma, informing him of the plan to free him.

As he sat back and let these thoughts run around in his mind, Sid began to relax. His momentary fears and doubts began to vanish. He had a feeling that everything was going to work out fine.

Fine for the Reece brothers, that was.

8

For a time he was back with the patrol, four days' ride from Fort Kane. Ten men, including Lieutenant Cale and himself, Sergeant Edwin Blaine, U.S. Cavalry. The purpose of the patrol was twofold. As well as keeping an eye open for any of the roving Apache renegades who were terrorizing the territory at the time, they also had the unenviable task of looking out for the band of white outlaws known as the Reece brothers. For quite a few years this gang of ruthless killers had been running wild. Nothing was too low for them if it promised a profit at the end. They sold guns and whiskey and even women to the Apaches. They rustled cattle, raided and looted, murdered and raped.

Two months back, one of the brothers had been caught. Sid Reece. And Edwin Blaine had been leading the patrol that had effected the capture.

Sid Reece had not given any indication as to the whereabouts of his brothers. Nevertheless, he had been tried and convicted. His sentence had been a long one. And he was to serve it in the territorial prison at Yuma.

Rumor, bar talk, or just plain gossip had it that Sid Reece's brothers would try to get him free before he reached Yuma Territorial Prison.

So a patrol left Fort Kane with others to watch out for the Reece brothers.

It didn't work out either way. No sign was seen of white or red man.

That was until a howling, screaming bunch of about thirty Apaches came drumming out of nowhere. Right into the middle of the weary line of dust-caked men and horses.

It was a short ugly fight. Blaine heard the thud of unshod hoofs, the sudden shouts of alarm, screams — both of pain and triumph. A ragged outburst of gunfire added its noise to the jarring cacophony of sound. Dust billowed up in choking yellow clouds.

Beside Blaine, Lt. Cale stiffened in his saddle. Blaine saw the two blood-gushing holes that appeared in the man's chest. Then, before Blaine could get his own gun up, there came a sudden red-hot explosion of pain in his back. Blaine's breath was slammed from his body by a terrific blow. His revolver slipped from numbed fingers. Jagged shafts of pain lanced through his body. He was aware of something hot and wet streaming down his back.

He felt himself toppling forward from his saddle. He tried to reach out and grab something; but there was nothing to grasp, and his hands and arms felt numb and useless. He saw the ground rush up at him. There was more pain as he struck; then all pain and all sound were cut off abruptly.

How long he lay there he never knew. He regained consciousness slowly, coming back to a world of pain and heat and silence. He lay still for a long time, waiting until his mixed-up senses slowly readjusted themselves into some semblance of order.

When Blaine finally moved, he felt a hot slash of pain boring into his back. He clenched his teeth and forced himself to a sitting position. The effort left him trembling and sobbing for air. Sweat poured down his dust-caked face. He sat motionless, almost afraid to move as he felt flickerings of pain darting around the burning spot in his back.

Even as he sat there he was making guesses as to what had hit him. It was no bullet or arrow wound, he decided. Judging by the way it hurt and the dragging weight, he reckoned he'd stopped an Apache lance. And when he felt over his shoulder, his probing fingers traced the outline of the lance-head, and followed the bloody shaft to where it had snapped off. *Must have broken when I fell*, he thought idly.

Abruptly his head snapped up. The goddamn Apaches.

But nothing moved or made a sound

near him. He was alone. Alone . . . save for the sprawling blood-streaked bodies of the patrol. Blaine glanced down at the body of Lt. Cale who lay only a few feet away. Cale's eyes were open wide as he stared blindly up at the sun. The once neat blue shirt was dark with dried, caked blood. Flies hovered over the chest wounds and crawled across the dead face. Blaine turned his face away. Next moment he was violently sick, choking harshly as he bent over.

An hour passed and Blaine was fifty yards from the scene of the ambush. This was as far as he had gotten.

He crouched in the shade of a low rock and pulled his hat down over his eyes. His breathing was dry and harsh, a rattling sound that began deep in his chest. He blinked his stinging aching eyes as sweat ran into them.

Even in his present state he was able to realize the fact he was alive was near enough to be called a miracle. Apaches usually made sure that no one was left alive after an attack, unless they were wanting prisoners. Blaine could only guess that the Apaches had been in a hurry, desperate for horses and ammunition. A swift, brutal attack which enabled them to run off the horses and then to vanish into the emptiness of the desert land where they could lose themselves quickly.

Blaine swore out loud. It did nothing for him. He managed a weak lopsided smile. *Well, Sergeant Edwin Oliver Blaine*, he asked himself, *is this your last fight? You've about used up all your chances. How many do you get? Maybe this is the one that leaves you a pile of bones somewhere out here.* Then Blaine shook his head angrily.

This was no way to be thinking. This wasn't him, it was the pain and the heat and the exhaustion that was leading him along these dark corridors of thought.

But even so he knew that his position was pretty grim.

He was alone, on foot, without food or water, shelter or weapons. He was also four days' distance from the fort.

And in his condition it was going to

be a long walk home.

If he had a horse things would be a lot easier. Blaine pushed the thought to the back of his mind and climbed slowly, painfully to his feet. He stood for a while trying to get his bearings. Finally he settled on heading south. The fort was somewhere in that direction.

He moved slowly, taking each step cautiously. The slightest jolt caused savage jabs of pain to drive deep into his shoulder.

He had been walking for a long time when he suddenly came face to face with the horse. A sorrel mare, carrying a cavalry saddle and gear. Blaine recognized it as one of the horses from the patrol. Its rider had been a young trooper named Collins. An eager, glory-seeking boy who now lay dead with his face shattered by a rifle slug, his blood soaked up by the dry, thirsty, indifferent land.

For a moment Blaine was too surprised to do anything.

The sorrel regarded him with respectful caution. It moved a few nervous steps as Blaine came toward it.

A deep grateful sigh slid past Blaine's lips as his fingers curled around the dangling reins. He leaned against the sorrel's side for a time until his strength allowed him to mount up. When he finally eased down into the saddle, he let go another sigh.

Blaine searched for a water canteen. There wasn't one. But the issue carbine was still in its leather case. The sight of it gave him a small amount of comfort.

At his command the sorrel moved off. He rode slowly.

There was no other way. He had to keep the horse moving without tiring it in a hurry. Blaine glanced up at the sky.

The sun continued to beat down on him without letup.

Blaine screwed up his face and pulled his hat low over his eyes. The pain in his back had now settled to a burning, nagging throb. Blaine began to sweat, and it wasn't all due to the heat of the sun.

Time ceased to be the thing that

measured the gaps between morning and noon and night; it became the moment he was burning hot; then the time he was bathed in cold torrents of sweat, his whole body shaking and trembling as if he were standing naked in a blizzard.

The last clear thing Blaine remembered doing was clenching his fists tight around the pommel. After that he was unaware of what took place, or how far he traveled, or where he came to . . .

* * *

Until, floating up out of a fathomless darkness, he opened his eyes and found he was lying on a bed in a small room with log walls. Blaine lay for long minutes, waiting for his thoughts to catch up with him.

He felt weak and, surprisingly, hungry. He became aware that his wound didn't hurt so bad now. And then he could feel the firm tightness of bandages round his chest.

Blaine abruptly realized what all this meant. He'd come out alive. He'd made it to somewhere. *Where?* He didn't know. Neither did he care. If he'd had the strength he would have raised the roof in thanks.

Instead he summoned up enough energy to call out, 'Hey! Anybody home?'

9

Katy was in the kitchen preparing food and coffee for the Reeces.

Ned Reece, a rifle in his hands, leaned against the wall watching her. His eyes roved over her body, probing, making her feel naked.

In the living room Chad was working with warm water and cloth on young Ham's face.

'I done what you said,' Jubal had said to Matthew.

Matthew Reece had pointed to Ham's trembling form. Then to a shocked Katy and Chad he said, 'Take a good look. Anybody steps out of line while we're here, they know what to expect. And that means you too, lady.'

Now, as he washed blood from his son's face, Chad had to fight down an urge to go for Jubal Reece and kill him.

But Chad kept his anger bottled up.

He knew that this was a time for waiting and also for calm, deliberate thinking.

Nothing could be gained by trying anything now. Except maybe, a bellyful of lead. Anyhow, even if he did manage to get outside, there was the young one to be faced. Hoby they called him. Chad knew the kind. Wild, kill-crazy, totally unpredictable. *No*, Chad decided, *I bide my time. Wait until a better chance comes along.*

Ham moved. A low groan came bubbling past his torn lips. His eyes opened slowly, painfully. He stared at Chad. 'Pa,' he said faintly.

Chad forced a smile on to his lips. 'All right, son. It's over now.'

'Pa, it hurts. Hurts awful.'

Chad nodded. He was trying to recall the last time Ham had called him Pa. *Must have been a hell of a while back*, he thought. Then he felt Ham's hand on his arm.

'What do they want, Pa?' Ham asked. 'Why've they come here?'

'We've come to meet a coach, boy,' Matthew Reece said. He stood beside Chad, gazing down at Ham.

'One of their brothers is being taken to Yuma prison on a special coach. These men intend to take him off the coach when it makes its halt here,' Chad explained.

Ham listened in silence. He felt Matthew Reece's eyes on him and rolled over on the couch he was stretched out on. Matthew laughed softly.

At that point Katy, followed by Ned, came into the room. She carried a loaded tray.

'About time,' Matthew snapped at her.

Katy gave him an angry look. 'You want to try cooking with that following you around,' she said sharply, nodding toward Ned Reece.

Matthew smiled, reached for the coffee. Ned scowled darkly.

'Careful, lady,' he warned.

Katy ignored him.

From the rear of the cabin came the voice of Edwin Blaine.

Katy turned. But Matthew blocked her way. 'Not so fast, lady. Jubal, keep your eye on these two. Ned, you come with me.'

Taking Katy's arm he pushed her roughly ahead of him, toward the room where Ed Blaine lay.

Blaine heard voices from beyond the door of the room.

Then footsteps came his way. Seconds later the door flew open with a bang. A woman stood there. Two men just behind her. The woman came into the room. One of the men came with her, a big, wide-shouldered man with a hard, tough face. The second man leaned against the door frame.

This, Blaine saw in the background. His attention was centered on the woman. For a moment he wondered if he were delirious. Wondered whether he was really awake.

Then he realized he was. His eyes were showing him the truth.

'Katy?' he said in wonderment. 'Katy?'

'Hello, Ed,' she said. And her voice was the same as he remembered it from before, warm and gentle, but firm and strong. She looked the same too, as she had always looked to him, a very lovely young woman. He remembered she was a bright, loving woman who could make a man feel half his age by just laughing.

But he noticed she wasn't laughing now. She was very far from it.

10

Matthew Reece broke the silence that had descended over the small room.

'Now ain't that a touching scene, Ned? Real touching.'

A laugh that was more a sneer came from Ned Reece.

Blaine heard this. And saw too the sudden rise of color in Katy's face.

'Friends of yours?' he asked, sensing that something was wrong.

Katy gave a sharp shake of her head. But before she could speak Matthew Reece strode around the bed. He stared down at Blaine.

'You might call us that,' he said. 'But I reckon the lady'll tell it different.'

'Truth is, soldier, she just don't like us,' Ned drawled as he moved into the room. He leaned himself against the end of the bed.

Being who he was, Blaine gave a

grunt of annoyance. He glanced across at Katy. 'Who are they, Katy? I'm in no mood for party games.'

Katy stared fixedly at Matthew Reece as she said, 'They're outlaws, Ed. There are four of them. They call themselves the Reece brothers.'

'My own fault for asking,' Blaine said. 'Out of the whole of Arizona I go and choose the spot where the Reece gang's hitched.' As an afterthought he asked, 'Anyhow, just where are we?'

Katy told him. Matthew Reece smiled coldly. 'Mister,' he said, 'you should have stopped out there.'

Blaine glanced from Matthew to the grinning Ned. He closed his eyes for a moment. Things were moving a little too fast for him in his present condition. Then he opened them again as a sudden thought struck him.

'What's the date?' he asked.

'It's the fourth today,' Katy told him.

Blaine nodded slowly. 'And they're moving your brother to Yuma,' he said to Matthew Reece.

81

'You hit it, soldier,' Ned said.

'Only you didn't say it quite right,' Matthew said. 'They are trying to get Sid to Yuma. They won't. Sid leaves that coach when it stops here and goes with us.' His voice hardened abruptly. 'I'll tell you too, soldier, like I told everybody here. I won't stand for anyone getting in the way. You try anything, you'll end up with a slug in you. The lady will tell you I'm not fooling.'

'They'll do it, Ed. They've already half-killed a young boy. For no reason.'

Matthew nodded at Katy's words. 'Convince him, lady,' he said.

He turned to Ned. 'Go out back, Ned. Keep an eye on our back trail, and watch this window. I don't think our friend will try anything, but you never know.'

Ned turned out of the room.

Matthew stood for a while, gazing down at the silent Blaine. 'Remember, lady, convince him I'm serious. And don't forget Ned's outside. I reckon you two have a few things to say to each other. Make it fast. When Sid gets here, I don't reckon you'll get another chance.'

He went slowly out of the room, closing the door behind him.

Blaine pushed himself awkwardly to a sitting position.

'You should rest,' Katy said absently.

He reached across and took her hands in his, ignoring the sullen throb in his shoulder. Gently he pulled her down on to the edge of the bed. 'I ought to bend you over my knee and give you a good dustin',' he said.

Katy looked at him, surprise in her eyes. 'For why?'

'Running off the way you did. Hell, why didn't you talk to me about it first?'

Katy shrugged her shoulders. 'Oh, you know how it is, Ed.'

'No, I don't. Anyhow you won't do it again. I asked you once to be my wife. You said yes. I'm holding you to that, no matter what you say now.'

'And what if I say no?'

'Just pretend I never heard you. Drag you off to the nearest preacher and marry you anyhow.'

She smiled at that.

'You look better when you do that,' Blaine told her.

'Not much to smile about at the moment. Ed, what can we do?'

'First,' Blaine said, 'this.'

He reached up and hooked his good arm round her neck, pulling her down to him. He felt the sweet, warm fullness of her lips on his, felt the short-lived resistance of her body. Then she relaxed against him, the soft mounds of her breasts warm through her thin shirt.

'Ed, oh, Ed,' he heard her say softly.

And though he was hoping to convince her otherwise, he was fast realizing that there was little he could do.

* * *

Inside the coach the heat was getting unbearable. It pressed in on the four men, wrapping itself around them like an invisible blanket.

McAllister leaned hard back in his seat and sweated. It dripped from his chin in a constant stream. He'd given up wiping the sweat off with his kerchief, since the square of cotton had become as wet as he was. He sat and sweated, feeling the clammy cling of his shirt and pants. Even his hands, that held his rifle, were moist and sticky. God, how he hated sweating like this. It made him irritable and jumpy.

Roll 'em up, Sam, begged McAllister silently. *Let's get to the station so we can get back to feeling human again.*

Hoby Reece made a thorough search of both cabin and barn, collecting any object he considered useful as a weapon. These things, along with the station's firearms, were put in an oak chest that stood in the main room. The chest was fastened with a hefty padlock, and Hoby pocketed the key. As he finished doing this, he caught sight of Chad watching him closely.

'Don't get any ideas, old man,' Hoby said. 'You get any notions about being brave, you have a look at your kid first.'

'Boy, if I catch you without that gun I'll kill you,' Chad said.

Something in his voice made Hoby pause, uncertain for a moment. Then the boy slapped the butt of his Colt.

'You don't scare me, pop,' Hoby said.

But Chad had noticed the uneasy pause, the fleeting break in Hoby's air of confidence, and he derived a small amount of satisfaction from it. He watched Hoby intently as the boy walked across the cabin and out of the door. Hoby paused outside and pulled the door shut with a bang. Chad glanced down at Ham who lay full-length on the couch.

Then he looked across at Jubal, sitting on a chair against the wall, motionless, his wide face empty of expression.

I won't forget you, either, bastard, Chad promised silently.

★ ★ ★

Even Harvy Martin was feeling the heat now. As the sweat ran down his face it traced a sharp biting path through the open gash left by Sid Reece's manacles. The knuckles of his right hand were raw and sore from slugging Reece's jaw. Hell, though, it had been worth it. Every time he leaned back and closed his eyes he could see again the figure of Sid Reece spinning away from his fist.

Ain't going to be no dirty prisoner ever getting the best of Harvy Martin, he promised himself. *Not while I got me two good fists and a cold, hard gun barrel.*

Through slitted eyes he peered at Sid Reece, noting with deep satisfaction the bruises that had formed on the outlaw's face.

Smiling to himself the lawman relaxed in his seat.

Suddenly the heat wasn't so bad. In fact Harvy Martin was feeling particularly good.

Sid Reece knew the young deputy kept looking at him. He paid no attention. He would have plenty of time for young Martin when the time came.

Yes sir, plenty of time.

Damnation, though, the coach is taking a hell of a time to reach Butler's Station. Hope the boys have everything ready for when we roll up. Of course they would. Matt would see to it. Hell, you ever known Matt to let you down? Quit worryin'. This time tomorrow you'll be long gone from around here.

Sid glanced across at Tom Peak. The deputy moved the barrels of his shotgun a fraction. Sid smiled and turned to look out the window. After a few minutes he closed his eyes and went to sleep.

Sam Loren was singing an old cowboy song he'd learned when he'd been a drover in his younger days. He'd forgotten a lot of the original words, but it made no difference since he used fresh lines each time he sang it.

He felt something tug his sleeve. Above the slap of the wind and the noise of the coach he could hear Will Hakin's voice.

'To the south, Sam. South.'

Swinging his head round Sam had a

momentary glimpse of a group of horsemen. Then they were gone.

'Who?' he yelled.

'Apache. I'm dead certain,' Hakin yelled back.

'That's all we need on this run,' Loren said. He hoped Will was wrong.

He began to haul in the team so he could pass on the news to his passengers. Hell, why should he do all the worrying?

11

They sat their sturdy ponies like carved brown statues. Only their eyes moved, black and bright, as they watched the distant shape of the Concord coach speeding across the empty land.

There were six of them. Clad in an odd assortment of clothing. One wore a tattered cavalryman's tunic, another wore *N'deh b'keh*, the traditional high-length Apache moccasins; breechcloth and the blue-checked top from a woman's dress. Yet another wore a filthy, blood-streaked, black frock coat. They all wore their black hair long, bound around the head with a broad strip of cloth.

At first glance they could have been mistaken for a group of slightly eccentric clowns. But anyone who made that assumption would change his mind in a hurry. Odd they may have looked, but they were no clowns. Nothing could have been further from the truth.

These were the Apache.

Deadly, swift-striking killers. A proud, fearless people, fighting a bloody war with the never-ending tide of white men who came into their sacred lands. Fighting to the death in a vain, toll-taking war as they tried to keep for themselves the land that had belonged to them before the *Pinda Lickoyi* ever set foot on the American continent.

Outnumbered, low on food, men and weapons, they were staging a last desperate stand. They resorted to hard-hitting, brutal attacks on anyone or anything likely to provide something useful. Maybe a raid would leave them with an extra rifle or a fresh horse. Many times they fought hard, lost warriors, and if the battle was theirs, found they had fought for nothing. But they carried on, for there was no other way for the Apache nation now. It was fight to live or die, since the time of words and promises was past. Too many times the smooth words of the white men had resulted in

91

the deaths of scores of Apaches . . . women and children as well as men.

So it was to an all-out war that the Apache dedicated himself. A war of no compromise, no mercy or quarter, no end except the ending that came with death.

And it was this situation that brought six Apache braves to this lonely spot, searching for something that might yield some booty to be carried in triumph to their camp.

One of the Apaches moved. He turned his head to look at his companions.

'Today the spirits bless us,' he said.

'Maybe, Chana,' one replied.

Chana gave a grunt of anger. 'Why do you always speak with darkness in your voice, Torrio?'

'He wishes to be home with his woman,' one of the group said.

'He wishes her to teach him basket-making,' said another.

Chana's brown face split into a near smile as he noted Torrio's black scowl.

'Have you lost heart, my friend?' he asked soberly.

Torrio shook his head. 'I have just gained great caution,' he said. 'It is not so easy to kill the *Pinda Lickoyi* any more. They have become good fighters. They do not give in to the Apache like they did in the old days. Now they have many good guns and much ammunition. The Apache have few guns, few bullets, few braves. Before we attack the coach we must plan and decide whether it is worth the risk.'

Chana nodded. He reached out and placed his hand on Torrio's arm.

'This one speaks wisely. What he says about the *Pinda Lickoyi* is true.' The others nodded their heads and motioned agreement.

Chana said, 'Then we shall follow the white man's coach. And we shall wait and then decide if it is in our favor to attack.'

He motioned with his arm and moved off. The others set their own mounts into action and fell into single file behind Chana as they began to trail the Concord across the scorching land.

Shortly, Chana sent one of his braves to alert the rest of the band who were awaiting his orders camped in a rocky basin six miles to the east.

★ ★ ★

Matthew Reece leaned up against one of the corral corner posts. His big-boned face was taut as he strained his eyes looking out over the wide plain.

He was beginning to get jumpy. It was a fault he had, one he knew of, yet was unable to cure. Waiting for something to happen, wondering about the outcome made his insides coil and harden. It was a bad thing, he knew. A man who let himself get emotionally upset was liable to make a mistake. And this particular time was not one for mistakes. Sid's life depended on the plan going smoothly, without mistakes of any kind. Any kind at all.

'Hey, Matt, you gettin' bellyache again?'

Matthew spun round. Hoby stood a

few feet away, a grin on his face.

'Why don't you keep your big mouth shut, boy,' Matthew said sharply.

Seeing he had gone too far Hoby wiped the grin from his face. He pulled off his hat and ran his fingers through his hair. He kept glancing at Matthew from the corner of his eyes.

'You give our horses a good rub down?' Matthew asked suddenly.

Hoby looked at him sharply. 'I ain't a damn stable-boy,' he said peevishly.

A huge arm swung up and round; Matthew's open hand struck Hoby across the side of his face, lifting him off his feet, then dropping him in the dirt.

Hoby hit the ground hard. He rolled and came up on one knee. His right hand dropped to his gun. Across his face was a large red welt.

'I'll kill you,' Hoby yelled. His voice was high and trembling, sounding childish and immature.

Matthew let him get to his feet. Even let him half draw his gun. Then he moved. Moved with a speed that was frightening for a man of his size.

As his brother closed in on him Hoby gave a squeal of fear. He looked wildly about him. His gun dropped back into its holster, forgotten, as Hoby flung up his arms to cover his face.

As his left hand grasped the front of Hoby's shirt, Matthew's right knocked the boy's arm aside. Then he began to slap Hoby's face with his open hand until the boy was crying like a baby.

'You've been asking for this a long time. I've been too damn soft with you. You listen, Hoby, 'cause I won't tell you again. You stay in line. Keep your mouth shut if you ain't got anything worthwhile to say. Understand?'

He waited until Hoby nodded.

'Now get over to that barn and make sure our horses are fit to travel. We're going to have a heap of riding to do shortly, and it ain't going to be handy if we're riding tired, broken-down mounts.'

Abruptly he released his hold on Hoby's shirt. Hoby fell to his knees and stayed there for a minute. Without raising his head he reached for his hat and jammed it on. Rising slowly to his feet, Hoby moved off toward the barn. He didn't look at Matthew.

There was a troubled look on Matthew Reece's face as he watched Hoby disappear into the barn. His hands were trembling and he clenched them tightly at his sides. He glanced toward the cabin. Jubal was standing in the open doorway. Matthew stared at him fixedly, and after a time Jubal backed slowly into the cabin and quietly closed the door: Matthew turned and gazed out over the wasteland again.

He slowly tilted back his head, letting his eyes roam across the burnished brassy-blue bowl of the sky. He felt the heat of the day on his face, and he squinted his eyes against the brightness of the sun. He took a deep breath, then exhaled. His body felt as taut as a drum skin. He felt he might go crazy if he couldn't release some of the tension that boiled inside him. And he felt a pang of guilt because he knew he had been taking some of it out on Hoby.

Hell, he thought, *what's wrong with me? Everything's working out fine. We're in charge here. And as soon as that stage gets here, we'll have Sid off and be away. So quit worryin'. Ain't nothing going to go wrong.*

But despite this self-assurance, Matthew Reece felt troubled. Even though he could not put his finger on it, he knew that something, somewhere, was going to make trouble for the Reeces.

* * *

'I hope Sam's wrong,' McAllister said. 'He ain't very often, but I hope he is this time.'

'Apaches,' Harvy Martin repeated softly. He spoke with the tone of a man who had heard the tales told about the Apache and their brutal ways, and suddenly realizes he might soon be face to face with them himself.

Sid Reece grinned knowingly. 'Scared, boy?' he asked.

98

Martin turned his gaze fully on the outlaw. 'Yeah. I'm scared.'

Sid held his stare for a moment. Then he muttered, 'Ah, the hell with you,' and lapsed into a sullen silence.

Tom Peak tilted his hat over his face to hide the grin he'd failed to hold back.

McAllister kept one eye on the skyline, hoping he wouldn't see what he was looking for.

They were three hours from Butler's Station.

12

His shoulder was coming to life again and it was making Blaine sweat. On the top of that he felt decidedly weak and light-headed. Katy kept telling him to lie down but Blaine refused.

'If I get my head on that pillow,' he said, 'it'll be a long time before I can get it off again.'

'Ed, you can be so stubborn.'

'That's why you love me,' he told her soberly. Then he asked her, 'How many of them are there?'

'Four. The two that were in here. Then there's a young one called Hoby. And the fourth is called Jubal. He's a big man, and a little . . . well, simple.'

Blaine nodded. 'I've heard about that one. You never know where you are with a feller like that. Still, we're not exactly picking partners for a dance.'

He glanced round the room, searching for something.

'Where are my clothes?'

'Those filthy things? I've put them away to be washed. Anyhow what do you want clothes for?'

Blaine turned his head to look at her. 'Because I'm getting up,' he said.

'Ed, you are not fit to get up. And have you forgotten there are four gunmen in the cabin, just waiting for you to put a foot in the wrong place? Do you want to get killed?'

He let her finish. Waited until she had no more words. 'Listen, Katy,' he said, 'I'm going to tell you this once and that's all. What you just said is true, I know. I also know there's a stage due here, with men aboard who don't know what's waiting for them here. They're going to walk right into a trap. And knowing the Reeces I'd say there'd be some dead men before they were done. No matter what, I can't sit here and let that happen. In a way I'm sort of responsible for this. I was the one who arrested Sid Reece in the first place. Now his brothers want him back. They'll do anything to free him. I've at least got to make an effort to stop them. Somehow . . . with or without your help.'

'With,' Katy said after a moment of strained silence.

'Okay. Now, how about some clothes?'

Katy went to a battered chest-of-drawers and produced a pair of pants and a faded blue shirt.

'Keep your eye on that feller outside,' Blaine said.

Katy glanced at the door. 'What if one of them comes in?'

'Let me worry about that.'

Katy crossed to the window. Ned Reece had wandered across to the creek. She watched him intently.

It seemed an eternity to Blaine before he got his feet off the bed and on to the floor. The effort cost him. It made him giddy. He sat still until his skull rejoined the top of his head. When he felt steady again, Blaine struggled into the shirt. It was a snug fit, but it would do. Getting into the pants proved more than a struggle. But, finally, he managed to get the belt buckled. His boots had been dropped beside the bed and Blaine dragged them on, pulling the pants down over the scratched and dusty leather.

Slowly Blaine stood. Moving steadily he found it wasn't too bad. But when he reached the door he was glad to lean against it for a moment.

'Katy?'

'He's still over by the creek, Ed,' she told him as she joined him.

'You ready?' he asked.

Katy nodded. 'Ed, do you know what you are doing?'

'At the moment I'm playing by ear,' he said. 'By necessity, not choice.'

He motioned her to open the door. Katy did so and stepped out into the passage. It was empty. From the main room came the muted tone of someone speaking, then a door slammed. Turning, Katy beckoned to Blaine. He stepped out and leaned against the wall, his face wet with sweat.

Keeping noise to a minimum they moved toward the curtained entrance to the main room. Their bodies were tight with tension, for they knew they might be spotted at any second. Ned Reece had only to glance through that solitary window and see that empty room. Blaine was waiting for the sudden shout, the explosive crash of a gun.

No warning had been sounded when they reached the hanging curtain. Blaine got himself positioned so that he could see past it and into the living room.

He saw Chad Butler crouching before a couch on which lay a boy of about twenty. The boy's face was a puffy, red-blotched mask. Blaine felt a sudden surge of anger directed against these men who for no logical reason had beaten up a mere boy.

He also saw, standing by the cabin's closed door, the one called Jubal. *God*, thought Blaine, *he is a big one*. There was no one else in the room, but through the front window he could see Matthew Reece. The man was leaning up against the station's big corral, staring out toward the empty plain. That had three of them placed for the moment. But where was the fourth? The young one called Hoby. He might just be outside the cabin door, waiting to burst in with a ready gun. Blaine pushed those kinds of thoughts to the back of his head. If he took into consideration all the things against him, he might just as well give up without trying. His only way was to take a chance with the situation as it was, and not as he wished it could be.

He could sense Katy standing very close to him. 'Katy,' he said softly, 'I want you to go in there and get Jubal's attention from this doorway. Give me time to get behind him.'

'But, Ed, what if one of the others comes in?'

'Honey, we've no time to be choosy. We'll just have to hope one of them *doesn't* come in.'

'But . . .'

Blaine's voice hardened suddenly. 'Do as I tell you, damn it.'

Color flooded Katy's cheeks. She dropped her eyes. 'All right, Ed.'

She moved past him slowly, shoulders held back, looking full ahead. Blaine reached out and touched her cheek with his fingers. 'Be careful,' he said.

Katy nodded and stepped forward, hesitating a moment before she passed into the living room.

Blaine edged to the door frame. He could see into the room without being observed himself. His gaze roved swiftly around the room, finally lighting on a stack of foot-long logs in the fireplace. If he could reach one and use it on Jubal before the big man could act, maybe, then, there'd be a chance.

As she stepped into the living room, Katy felt a moment of absolute panic. *I can't do it*, she told herself. Then just as quickly she argued, *yes you can. You must. For Ed. For Chad and Ham. And for those men on the stage.* Though her legs threatened to collapse, she moved forward. She knew she was trembling and hoped it wasn't noticeable.

Chad spotted her first. He looked at her with a puzzled expression on his face. Katy gave a quick shake of her head. Deliberately, she knocked against a chair. At the sound Jubal spun round. His thick eyebrows rose in a deep frown.

'What you doin'?' he asked.

'I don't feel too well,' Katy answered on the spur of the moment. And it wasn't far from the truth.

'*Uh?*' Jubal grunted. His small eyes were fixed on Katy, unblinking.

'Maybe I could go outside for some fresh air.'

'Have to ask Matt,' Jubal said.

He turned and headed for the door. Katy realized this was no good. She had to do something fast to keep him from calling Matthew Reece. Giving a wailing sigh, she let herself slump to the floor at Jubal's feet.

'She's fainted,' Katy heard Chad say.

She sensed Jubal getting to his knees beside her. *Hurry, Ed, hurry. For God's sake hurry*, she cried mentally.

The instant Katy stepped into the living room, Ed Blaine wished she were still at his side. *Mister*, he told himself, *you ain't done much prayin' in your time, so make up for it now.*

But Jubal was heading for the door. Blaine realized what was going to happen. He gauged the distance to the pile of logs on the hearth.

Could he reach them before Jubal got to the door?

Then, almost magically, Katy was sprawled on the floor, Jubal turning back and kneeling beside her.

This was it, Blaine knew. He shoved through the door without hesitation. Four unsteady steps took him within reaching distance of the logs. He chose one he could close his hand over. He turned, forced his weak legs to carry him across the room. As he came up behind Jubal he raised the log in his hand, brought it down hard across Jubal's skull.

A grunt of pain mingled with anger broke from Jubal's lips. His great head swung round, his eyes settled on Blaine. Jubal touched a hand to where Blaine had hit him.

His fingers came away sticky with blood.

Blaine swung back his club for a second blow as Jubal pushed to his feet. The huge clawing hands reached out for Blaine . . . the fingers of one catching his face . . . then the log came down. The slamming blow took Jubal between the eyes. Jubal gave a groan of pain. He brought both hands up to cover his face. Blaine stepped aside as Jubal fell like a toppled tree. He hit the floor and lay still.

'Well done, soldier,' Chad grinned as he helped a white-faced Katy to her feet.

'Any weapons? Blaine asked shortly.

'Ah, they collected all of them and

put them in that oak chest over there,' Chad told him.

Blaine crossed over to the chest, knelt beside it. Anger rose in his throat as he saw the heavy padlock that fastened the lid down.

'Katy, get me a poker.'

Katy searched among the fire irons and brought him a thick, heavy length of iron. Blaine took it and jammed one end behind the metal hasp. He began to lever against the pull of the six long screws that held it tight in the hard wood.

Chad added his two hands to Blaine's one. The hasp creaked gently. The poker began to bend under the pressure.

Blaine started to sweat again. Chad began to swear.

Wood groaned, then cracked. The hasp slowly began to lift away from the chest. Then the poker slid from behind the hasp, suddenly, without warning. Blaine put out a hand to steady himself and felt sharp streaks of pain in his shoulder. Ignoring the pain and the feeling of sickness that threatened to engulf him, Blaine savagely rammed the poker back into position.

From somewhere outside came an angry shout. Katy shot an anxious glance at Blaine.

'Here comes trouble,' Chad muttered. He pushed Blaine out of the way and exerted his full strength on the poker.

Under his forceful attack the hasp finally gave in.

Something snapped. Metal screeched. The hasp and lock clattered to the floorboards. Blaine fumbled with the chest's heavy lid. He raised it, threw it back.

Footsteps sounded, approaching the cabin fast.

Blaine reached inside the chest and grabbed a long-barreled Colt .45. He checked it and found it was fully loaded.

The cabin's front door flew open with a crash.

Blaine rose to his feet, turning and thumbing back the hammer on the Colt. As he began to raise the gun, he saw someone step through the door he'd entered a minute back. It was Ned Reece. He held a leveled rifle.

'If you want the lady to stop a few slugs, you just go ahead and use that thing,' Matthew Reece said from his position just inside the front door. His own gun was trained directly on Katy. Anger rose again in Blaine's throat. So damn near, he thought bitterly. He glanced at Katy. She was facing Matthew Reece squarely, though her face was white and tense.

Blaine felt his finger pressing on the trigger. Had he a chance? He knew the answer was no. Had he been alone it might have been different. But he held three other lives in his gun hand, and there was only one thing he could do.

'We ain't waitin' all day, soldier,' Ned Reece said. He moved into the room, his rifle on Blaine.

Blaine let the hammer down. He relaxed his grip on the trigger. This time they had him cold. No use in trying to play the hero and ending up dead and useless. He let the Colt slip from his fingers. It hit the floor at his feet.

'Now, just you kick that over here, friend,' Matthew said.

He moved into the room and walked slowly across the floor, his cold, hard eyes on Blaine every inch of the way.

His face was stiff and set, looking like a carved wooden mask. He stopped a couple of feet away from Blaine. He bent and picked up Blaine's gun.

'You, friend, are either a fool or a damn clever man,' he said softly.

And then the gun in his hand rose sharply, glinting wickedly as a shaft of sunlight caught it before it slashed down at Blaine's face.

★ ★ ★

The rest of Chana's warriors joined up with the scouting party an hour's ride from Butler's Station. Now they were twenty strong. All were tough, tried fighters, impatient for action after long weeks of waiting and hearing of the victories of other bands. Only two days ago a band of thirty warriors had attacked and slaughtered a patrol of the blue-shirted pony-soldiers. The warriors of Chana wanted a victory of their own now.

At this moment, though, they hunkered down in the hot sand, watching the progress of the coach far below their high vantage point.

Chana stood aside from the others, his face grim as he followed the movement of the distant Concord. He had a decision to make. Should he lead his braves to attack the coach, or should they search for better game? An attack could mean loss of life for many of the warriors. And even if victory was theirs, the coach might only yield a small reward.

The Apache nation was going through hard times now. They had little food, poor land, and were becoming desperate in their fight for survival. Treaties had been made with the white man, only to be broken by his greed and treachery. In a final attempt to regain all that was rightfully his, the Apache had declared all-out war on the whites. But to do this the Apache still had to eat, drink, live, and keep himself mounted and armed.

These things and many more passed through Chana's mind as he tried to decide what he should do. The coach might be carrying things the Apache needed. Food, maybe even guns and ammunition. Was the risk worth it?

Would Chana and his warriors be changing their lives for nothing, or would they gain much-needed weapons and supplies for their fight against the whites?

Chana gave a grunt of frustration. 'Torrio,' he called.

Silently Torrio padded up to his leader. His bright eyes scanned Chana's set features. He placed a hand on Chana's shoulder.

'A man must make his decision and stand firm by it, my brother,' he said.

Chana glanced at him and nodded.

Torrio was indeed a good companion. In the friendship they had shared since boyhood, Chana found in Torrio a wise and capable counselor. He was able to voice his thoughts to Torrio and receive advice given by a man of sound, deliberate judgment.

'Would it not be good if we returned home with our arms holding the spoils of the victory?' Chana asked. 'Even if it were only a small victory,' he added.

'Then Chana has decided to attack?'

'The warriors grow restless with no fighting. Even this,' indicating the distant coach, 'small prize is better than none at all.'

Torrio squatted in the dust at Chana's feet. He studied the cloud of dust that wormed along behind the coach.

'Beyond the hills lies the place called Butler's Station where the *Pinda Lickoyi* rest their horses. The coach will stop there.'

Chana listened intently.

'You are my eyes and ears, Torrio. I

would be as an unborn child without you.' He smiled one of his rare smiles, his teeth flashing white against his dark skin.

'Then we shall attack when the coach stops at the resting place and destroy all we find there. Come, Torrio, watch how the light returns to the dull eyes of my warriors when I tell them of my decision.'

Within minutes the silent band of dark-skinned warriors was mounted and they were once more trailing the speeding Concord.

13

It took Katy a long time to stop the bleeding from the gash on Blaine's cheek, laid open by the front sight of the gun in Matthew Reece's hand.

'Did you have to do that?' Katy had asked as Blaine had fallen to his knees.

Matthew shook his head. 'No,' he said. 'I didn't have to do that. I could have killed him.'

Now they sat in silence around the cabin.

Blaine sat on a chair beside the big table in the center of the room. He felt weak and sick again. He'd lost more blood than he could afford. And the blow had taken a lot out of him. This, on top of all his actions since getting out of bed, had drained away the reserve of his strength. His shoulder was throbbing wildly again. He could feel cold beads of sweat on his face and guessed he must look a miserable sight.

He could feel the eyes of the Reece clan on him. They were all in the cabin now. Hoby was on watch by the window. Ned was keeping close to Jubal, for the big man was in a dangerous state. Only Matthew's command had kept him from attacking Blaine. He sat across the room from Blaine, but never took his eyes off him. Every so often Jubal would raise a huge hand and rub the livid bruise on his forehead.

Matthew Reece sat across the table from Blaine watching Katy work on the gash he'd opened. Blaine tried to read the thoughts that coursed through Matthew's head.

He failed. With most people, Blaine had learned you could work out a little of what they were thinking by looking at their eyes. But this was impossible with Matthew Reece. His eyes were expressionless, devoid of any emotion. So too was his face.

'You won't get medals for fool stunts like that,' he said suddenly.

'We almost pulled it off,' Chad Butler said, ignoring the gun pointed at him by Ned Reece.

'And almost got your belly full of lead,' Matthew snapped back at him.

'You expect us to sit back and let you go ahead without trying to stop you?' Blaine asked. His voice came out harsh and bitter.

'You've got no stake in this, Blaine. Why interfere?' Matthew questioned.

Blaine shook his head. 'You wouldn't understand, Reece.'

'So try me, friend.'

'Okay. Reece, as long as your kind is around there'll be somebody to stop you. Sure, you say why interfere? Why not keep out of sight and pretend it's not really happening? I could do that. So could a lot of other people in similar situations, just ignore all the killing and destroying. Let them trample down everything worthwhile that's been built out here. That's how you'd like it, Reece. A free run for you and your worthless kind. But it won't work.

People are trying to build a new country out here. People who are too proud and stubborn to let you run over them. I like to include myself in that category. Like I say, Reece, your way just won't work.'

Matthew Reece sat quite still. He had listened carefully to Blaine, digesting all that had been said.

From the other side of the room Hoby called, 'Soldier, you ought to be the damn president. Man what a speech.'

'Shut your ignorant mouth,' Matthew said. He spoke without taking his eyes off Blaine.

Hoby fell silent, automatically raising his hand to his bruised face.

'Much as I don't agree with your sentiments, mister, I got to admit I kind of admire a man who has so much faith in his belief.' Matthew sat back in his chair, and for a second Blaine thought he saw a fleeting smile cross the hard face. 'But don't get any ideas. You foul me up and I'll kill you. I mean it. I aim to get my brother Sid off that coach.

Anybody who gets in my way will have to take what comes along.' He raised his voice. 'You all hear this. I told you before, I'll tell you again. Nobody get in the way unless they're tired of life. Tread careful.' He turned to his brothers. 'The coach is getting mighty close now. I don't want any slips. From now on if one of these people makes a move that looks out of place, you don't wait. You've got guns. Use them.'

He let it sink in. Then he stood up. Glanced down at Blaine.

'I stand by what I say, too, mister. That's why I'm still alive.'

Outside it was still hot. Heat waves shimmered hazily across the parched land. Nothing moved. No sound broke the grave-like stillness. It was as if the very land itself was waiting for something to happen. Something that would shatter the stillness and silence with its fury and sudden violence.

14

As time passed the tension in the coach heightened to such a pitch that the slightest move in the wrong direction could have caused an explosion.

Marshal McAllister was suffering badly from the pain in his back. It was beginning to show on his face now, and in his speech and actions. The more he tried to ignore it the worse it got.

Under the pretext of going to sleep he closed his eyes and sank down in his seat. *God*, he thought, *we'd better reach the station fast. I can't stand much more of this. I don't care how tough I'm supposed to be. I need to get out of this damned contraption before it kills me.*

He pushed aside the pain for a minute and tried to picture the ranch where he'd live as soon as this job was over. And to hell with riding and having to make camp out in the back of beyond; and roaming round the country with dirty, ignorant killers who had to be shifted from one jail to another. He would forget all that when he handed in his badge. And that couldn't be soon enough.

Of the four men in the coach the most alert was Harvy Martin.

He was straight and stiff in his seat. He watched and listened. His mind raced wildly as he tried to keep watch out of both sides of the coach and not lose sight of Sid Reece.

Martin was almost praying for something to happen.

Ever since the exhilarating moment when his fist had smashed against Reece's face, he'd been filled with the desire to be able to use his gun. It was a feeling that drew him up taut, left him keyed up ready for anything. But it was a dangerous condition to be in; it gave a man false confidence; made him cocky and self-assured when he was, in fact, over-reaching his actual capabilities.

But to Harvy Martin it was fine. He

felt ready to tackle anything. Be it the Reece brothers or the Apache, give him a chance to use his gun, and he'd show who was top man.

And if he had his way, the first to stand before his muzzle would be Sid Reece.

Sid Reece was feeling free already. The nearer they got to Butler's Station, the easier he felt. He wasn't worried about anything going wrong. Not with Matt in control. He knew Matt well enough to have that much faith in him.

Sid glanced down at the chains on his wrists and legs. Somebody was going to suffer when he got them off, that he promised. His wrists were chafed raw by the rough bands of iron. *Yes, sir, some bastard is going to suffer.* Sid raised his eyes to Harvy Martin's face. Some bastard.

The Concord rattled on its dusty way toward Butler's Station.

Its occupants, though watchful, were unable to spot the band of horsemen who were trailing the coach.

Chana and his warriors rode at an easy pace. They could have overtaken the coach at any time. But they were content just to keep it in sight and follow. There was no hurry. They were very patient. They could wait. Time was important only to the whites, it meant nothing to the Apache. All they had to do was to wait for the right moment. When it came they would strike swift and sure. They would be on the whites before anything could stop them.

15

Hoby spotted the coach as it crested a rise half a mile from the station.

'Matt, it's coming.'

Matthew crossed over to the window and watched the approaching coach. 'Stay here,' he told Hoby.

He turned back across the room, pointing at Chad. 'Butler, when that coach pulls in you go out like you do normally. Do the usual things, no more. Just act natural. You'd better because your boy, the girl and the soldier are going to be in here with a gun on them. You mess this up and they die. Understand?'

Chad nodded. 'I understand. But you harm any of them people and I'll kill you myself.'

Matthew smiled bleakly, without humor. 'Soldier, your speech has caught on. Everybody's making threats.' He turned to Hoby. 'I want you in the barn. Don't do a thing till I make my move. Then come out fast.'

'Okay, Matt.'

'Ned, I want you to stick by our friends here. Watch them close. Don't give them any chance to pull a thing.'

Ned Reece nodded.

Matthew picked up two rifles and checked them both carefully. He handed one to Jubal. The big man took the gun very gently in his huge hands.

'I want you to stick with me, Jubal. Do what I tell you and don't ask any questions. Okay?'

'All right, Matt.'

'Everybody knows what's what now. Any questions?'

Matthew looked round the room. He stopped at Katy. 'You lost that busy tongue, ma'am?'

'Leave her alone,' Blaine said sharply.

'It's all right, Ed,' Katy said. She glanced coolly at Matthew. 'I've no words to waste on you, Reece.'

Matthew touched his hat brim.

'Thank you, ma'am,' he said mockingly. Then he turned his back on her. 'Hoby, you get out to the barn. And remember what I said.'

Matthew watched his younger brother move swiftly across the yard. He waited until Hoby vanished into the barn's shadowed doorway. Then he turned to face the room again.

'You three, get across to that wall and sit on the floor with your hands in sight. Ned, stay with them. Butler, you get outside and make like you're working. And don't get smart.'

Chad threw a despairing glance toward Blaine.

'Go ahead,' Blaine told him. 'They've got all the guns at the moment.'

As Chad headed outside, Ham called after him, 'Be careful, Pa.'

Matthew closed the door and joined Jubal at the window.

They could see Chad over by the corral. They watched as he started to dig a hole for a new corner post.

They waited in silence.

Heat descended like a smothering blanket. Sweat formed on their bodies. From heat and tension and fear.

Somewhere in the cabin a fly began to buzz angrily.

The sound of Chad's digging was faint, and somehow out of place with the situation.

In the cabin the heat was getting steadily worse. The buzzing fly had found a partner and they were both making noise now.

Then faintly came the unmistakable sound of horses pulling a heavy wheeled vehicle. The sound grew until they could make out the many individual noises that made up the familiar cacophony. The dull thud of many hoofs; the rattle of iron-rimmed wheels; the jingle and creak of harness and trappings. And then the sound rose in volume as the Concord swept into the yard, coming to a creaking, plunging halt before the cabin. Dust billowed up around the coach, momentarily obscuring Matthew Reece's vision. But it was gone in seconds, and he could see Chad walking toward the coach.

'Ready, Jubal?'

Jubal nodded. 'Ready, Matt.'

* * *

Sam Loren wrapped his reins round the brake-handle and swung himself to the ground. He saw Chad Butler coming across the yard.

'Hi, Chad, you old son.'

'Good to see you, Sam.' Chad tried to sound as though he meant it.

Loren realized something was wrong. He knew when Chad spoke, could tell by the strained expression on Chad's face.

'Chad, you got trouble?'

Chad stiffened visibly. He glanced over his shoulder toward the cabin. Then he shook his head slightly and looked at Loren.

'I . . . you see, Sam . . . we had an accident. Ham got a leg broke. He's in bed. I'm just tired, I guess. What with

trying to keep things going and all.'
Chad hoped he sounded convincing.

Sam Loren glanced toward the cabin.
'Sure am sorry, Chad. Hard on you.'

He turned to the coach.

'Marshal, you can light down now.'
He took Chad aside. 'Got a marshal
and a couple deputies taking a prisoner
to Yuma. Feller called Sid Reece.'

'I heard about him,' Chad said. He
moved up to the front of the coach and
began to check the shoes on one of the
lead horses.

Sam Loren followed, puzzled by
Chad's lack of interest in such a
notorious outlaw as Sid Reece.

Before they got out of the coach
McAllister said, 'I don't want a repeat
of what happened out there. Understand?'

Harvy Martin nodded too quickly.
McAllister sensed he'd have to watch
the boy closely.

Tom Peak settled his hat firmly and
said, 'There'll be no trouble.'

Sid Reece gave a mocking laugh. 'No

trouble, Marshal, sir.'

Shoving open the door McAllister eased his aching body out of the coach. The heat was just as bad out here. Worse if anything. He leaned up against the side of the coach, propping his rifle beside him. He glanced toward the cabin. *It sure does look cool in there*, he thought, as he let his gaze rove past the deep-shadowed window. Cool and quiet.

Very quiet.

Too quiet.

McAllister forgot his aching body, forgot about the heat and dust and sweat as a feeling of foreboding swept over him. Something was way out of line, he decided. And as he always had before, McAllister acted on impulse.

'Get him back inside, Tom,' he yelled to Peak. Without question the deputy shoved Sid Reece off the step, back inside the coach.

McAllister reached for his weapon. As his fingers closed round it, two men with rifles burst out of the suddenly opened cabin door.

From above him McAllister heard the voice of Will Hakin yell: 'Marshal, by the barn,' followed by the boom of a shotgun.

McAllister raised his rifle, swung it up and round, working the lever. He heard a sudden burst of gunfire very close to him. Someone shouted, but he was unable to make out what was said. The coach swayed as the team moved restlessly.

Before McAllister could pull the trigger of his rifle, he felt a powerful blow in his stomach. It took his breath away. He banged up against the rear wheel of the jerking coach. He let his suddenly heavy rifle drop from his fingers. His hat fell off and bounced as it hit the ground. His stomach hurt him badly; it felt as if a rod of red-hot iron had been jabbed into him. A second slug slammed into his chest. McAllister's head fell forward on to his chest and he was shocked to see a huge wet, spreading patch of red staining his shirt and pants.

My God, I've been shot, he realized very calmly. He hung there against the side of the coach, watching his blood pump out of the hole in his stomach. His eyes filled with tears as he fell to his knees, but his mind was surprisingly clear. And he realized he would never see the ranch up at Bisbee, or his grandson. A rattling cough burst from his chest, erupting in a scarlet rush of blood from his mouth. He fell on to his face, dead before he hit the ground.

* * *

The instant he saw the old marshal reach for his gun Matthew said, 'Let's go, Jubal.' He swung open the door and ran in a crouch, out into the naked glare of daylight. From the corner of his eye he saw Hoby come out of the barn.

Up on the coach the guard let go with his shotgun. Dust kicked up close to Hoby's feet. Matthew raised his rifle and triggered off two shots. The guard let go of his shotgun and clasped both hands to his shattered face. He twisted to one side and plunged blindly off the top of the coach. When Sam Loren made to resist Matthew put a shot into his arm.

Jubal's rifle sounded and the marshal took a slug in the stomach and a second in the chest.

A gun spoke from inside the coach and the slug nicked Matthew's left sleeve. Matthew dropped to one knee, raising his rifle toward the coach.

As he did the door flew open and a figure was flung out.

Matthew dropped the muzzle of his rifle and aimed it at the man who lay sprawled in the dust before him.

★　★　★

Sid Reece caught a glimpse of Matthew and Jubal as they came out of the cabin. Then Tom Peak shoved him roughly into the coach. Peak threw himself after the outlaw and pulled the door shut.

Harvy Martin was kicking open the door on the other side as the dull boom of gunfire began.

Peak started shooting through one of the side windows.

Though hampered by the manacles he wore, Sid Reece was still able to handle himself. He threw his full weight against Tom Peak. The deputy was catapulted through the coach door, out on to the yard.

Half out of the coach, on the other side, Harvy Martin saw Reece's move. He pushed back into the coach, swinging his gun at Sid's head. But Sid ducked beneath the weapon. Recovering his balance, Sid swung his clenched fists at Martin's face. As his fists struck hard across Martin's jaw, Sid threw his full weight against the deputy. They smashed hard against the door Martin had been about to leave the coach by. The door was torn from hinges and frame as the two men fell through in a fighting tangle.

They hit the ground hard, spilling

apart, coming to their feet fast. For a moment they eyed one another, their lungs heaving as they sucked air. Martin moved in first, his arms reaching out before him. He looked confident, as if he were the victor already. His right fist slashed at Sid's head, but met only empty air. Sid, showing amazing speed for a manacled man, had stepped back out of reach. Then before Martin could set himself for another blow, Sid stepped in close and sank both fists deep into Martin's stomach. The deputy gave a grunt of pain and fell back a step. There was something shockingly brutal about the way Sid moved in and methodically began to beat Martin to his knees. Twice the deputy slumped to the ground. Sid just reached and hauled him upright again. And when Martin was unable to hold himself up, Sid used his boots. If the chains round his ankles hadn't restricted the force of the blows, Martin would have taken a terrible beating. As it was he lay in the dust, barely moving when Sid finally drew back, a satisfied smile on his sweat-streaked face.

'You wanted to play rough, boy. I reckon you're obliged,' Sid said softly.

Abruptly a heavy hand closed over Sid's shoulder. Sid's head snapped round. He looked into the face of his brother Matthew.

'Hello, Sid.'

'Matt, it's damn good to see you,' Sid roared.

Matthew smiled, then the welcome over he said, 'Let's get those damn chains off you first.'

They moved round to the other side of the coach.

Matthew knelt beside the dead marshal and began searching for the keys that would unlock Sid's manacles.

'He dead too?' Sid asked. He indicated the sprawled form of Tom Peak.

Matthew rose with the keys in his hand. 'No. I just let him feel the end of my gun barrel.'

He unlocked the manacles from Sid's hands and feet. Sid took them, weighed them in his hands a moment, then threw them hard away from him. He saw Matthew watching him and laughed.

'Sort of took a dislike to them damn things,' he said, rubbing at the raw bands of flesh on his wrists.

'Hey, Sid!'

Sid turned to see Hoby grinning at him. Hoby had Sam Loren and Chad under his gun. The stage driver was nursing a bloody left arm.

'Hello, little brother,' Sid grinned back.

Jubal appeared from behind the coach. He was half-dragging, half-walking Harvy Martin. As he spotted Sid, he gave Martin a shove that sent the deputy sprawling into the dust at Sid's feet.

Jubal said, 'We done it, Sid. We done it.'

'Sure you did. I knew you wouldn't let me down.'

Matthew rubbed his unshaven jaw. 'Sid, let's get inside. We could all do with something to drink. Then we'd better make plans. I got some ideas I want you to hear.'

'Yeah, I could do with a drink.'

Before they went inside, they placed the bodies of McAllister and the guard inside the coach. Then Hoby drove the coach toward the barn.

Sid picked up some of the fallen guns. He prodded Martin to his feet. The deputy was still in a dazed state, barely able to make out what was happening.

'You two, get him on his feet,' Sid said to Chad and Sam Loren, pointing at Tom Peak.

Under Matthew's watchful gaze the two men hauled Peak upright and assisted him into the cabin.

'Jubal, make sure there are no guns left lying around out here,' Sid said. He gave Martin a shove. 'Inside, tough guy.'

It was hot in the cabin. Ned had opened the window but it hadn't made much difference. Sid pushed Martin through the door and stood in the opening for a minute.

He let his gaze rove freely round the

room. His eyes lingered hungrily on Katy, and he grinned at the hostile stare she gave him. Then he passed her and let his eyes drop to the man who sat beside her. A big man, who looked as though he'd recently taken some rough punishment. The face was somehow familiar. Sid stepped into the room so he could get a closer look at the man's face.

Then it hit him. And he wondered how he could have forgotten so quickly.

'By God! Ed Blaine. I reckoned on having a long wait before I settled with you.'

His gun rose and centered on Blaine. There was madness in Sid's eyes as he thumbed back the hammer.

16

Two miles from the station Chana halted his band. The warriors dismounted, found shade for their ponies and themselves and squatted, silent and still, awaiting the command of their leader.

Chana drew Torrio aside and they shared a drink from Chana's water skin.

'First, I will send a scout to see how strong this place is,' Chana said. 'When he returns, we shall decide what to do.'

'It is wise,' Torrio said.

'Good. Then who shall I send? Masai is a good scout. Santria, too.'

'Only one here is able to do it correctly. To learn the things you will want to know,' Torrio said solemnly.

Chana looked at his companion closely.

'I will go,' Torrio said.

'*No!*' Chana said too sharply.

'Does Chana think I am now too old to do this? Am I only to sit by his side and offer him words?'

'No, my friend. There are none who can better you.'

'Then I shall go.' Torrio considered his leader, his friend, gravely. 'I will return, Chana. We have many battles to fight yet.'

He rose and padded to his pony. Chana followed him. Watched him mount up. Chana's face was lined with concern.

'Be ready for my return,' Torrio said.

Chana put a hand to Torrio's arm. 'Take care, my brother. I have bad feelings about this day.'

'Chana, you become an old woman,' Torrio laughed.

He kicked his pony into motion, the animal picking its sure-footed way among the rocks that dotted the ground.

Chana watched until Torrio vanished from his sight.

'May the spirits stay at your side,' he said.

He squatted on his heels and stared at the ground. The feeling he had spoken of to Torrio grew with every second that passed.

★ ★ ★

Torrio dismounted from his pony when he was within five hundred yards of the station. Armed with only a knife he moved swiftly and silently toward the station.

He used extreme caution in his approach, for when he had been still a good way off, he had heard the sound of gunshots. They had been faint, but unmistakable.

Now, as he lay on his stomach, only fifty yards from the corral, Torrio wondered what had happened. The station looked completely deserted. Nothing moved. No sound reached him. The coach was not in sight. Had the *Pinda Lickoyi* fought among themselves as they often did? Had they already left? Torrio wished he had the answer. Maybe the whites knew about Chana's band. Perhaps this was a trap. Maybe the whites waited inside the cabin. And when the Apaches rode in . . .

Torrio decided to have a closer look before he went back to Chana.

He began to work his way in toward the corral.

* * *

Hoby had maneuvered the big clumsy Concord into the barn. Climbing down from the box, he unhitched the team and led the horses into separate stalls. By the time he had them all fed and watered he was sweating. This kind of work was not in Hoby's book.

Hoby headed for the door and fresh air. He was still in the deep shadow that lay around the entrance when his sharp, alert eyes caught a flicker of movement out beyond the corral. Hoby froze. He watched the spot carefully. He knew he hadn't imagined it. Something or someone was out there. Hoby took off his hat and used it to shade his eyes. Now he could make out a vague shape. The shape took on form and color.

It was a man. Not white. An Indian. An Apache.

'A goddamn Apache,' Hoby breathed. Then he thought, *Here's one buck who won't lay with his squaw tonight.*

Hoby put his hat back on and dropped his hand to his Colt. He wondered what this lone brave was doing out here. But he didn't take it any further. It was the biggest mistake of his life.

Stepping to the nearest stall, Hoby led the horse out.

He paused at the door, then started out into the sunlight, heading toward the corral, walking unhurriedly. He kept the horse between himself and the Apache.

★　★　★

Torrio was close to the corral when he saw the white man lead the horse out of the barn. The Apache froze where he was. Only his eyes moved as they followed the progress of the man and horse across the yard. On reaching the corral the man opened the gate and led the horse inside.

Torrio saw the man release the horse, then turn away to go out of the corral. The man took only two steps. Then he spun round and looked straight at the spot where Torrio lay. In his hand was a gun. Torrio saw a flash of red blossom from the black muzzle.

As the Colt slapped against his palm, Hoby saw the Apache jerk sideways. He ran to the corral fence and slipped through. He thought his shot had missed, but now he could see a patch of red streaking the Apache's left shoulder. Hoby tripped the trigger again. The Apache clutched his stomach, blood seeping through his fingers. Hoby halted a few feet away from the Apache and grinned.

'You take a lot of killing, friend,' he said, and pulled the trigger again.

The Colt gave only a dull click. Hoby

148

swore. Christ, he'd had no time to reload since they'd taken over the coach.

The Apache was pushing to his feet. For a moment Hoby stood helpless, his empty gun hanging uselessly from his fingers. Then he realized he held the weapon and he brought it up to hit the Apache.

He was seconds too late.

The Apache's right arm swept up above his head.

Something flashed coldly in the sunlight, then the arm descended. Hoby felt a slamming blow on his chest, followed by a searing shaft of pain that ripped a scream of terror from his lips. Hoby clawed at the object of his pain and felt his hands grow wet and sticky. He could see it now.

The worn handle of a knife, the blade of which was buried deep in his chest. Hoby's legs gave way and he fell on to his back. He lay in the dust, his arms and legs kicking and jerking. All reason left him as he tried to rid himself of the agonizing pain in his chest. He only made things worse. The harder he thrashed about, the faster his blood pumped from the gash in his flesh. But Hoby realized none of this, he knew only of pain he'd never dreamed of, his mind was unable to accept anything else. He was an animal in pain, and he didn't know how to stop that pain.

So he clawed at his chest and thrashed about in the dirt, hoping it would make the pain stop. And he screamed, because he was frightened and had to do something. So he screamed. Until blood flooded his throat and almost choked him.

★　★　★

Torrio crawled the last few feet to where his pony stood.

He knew the men from the station were close behind him. He had seen them burst out of the cabin as his attacker had fallen to the ground with Torrio's knife in his chest. It had taken all of Torrio's strength to keep him on his feet as he turned and ran. He was hit badly. The shoulder wound was nothing. But the second bullet had lodged deep inside and done much damage. He was bleeding badly. But as long as he had breath in him, he would keep moving.

His pony, trained to ignore the scent of blood, stood motionless as Torrio dragged himself on to its back. As he kicked the pony into motion Torrio heard the crackle of gunfire. Some shots came very close. But before the white men could get within proper range Torrio was gone, his pony carrying him swiftly into the empty land where the Apache was master at losing himself in the sandy, trackless wastes.

17

For the second time that day Ed Blaine found himself staring death in the face. Death in the form of a cocked gun aimed at his head. He heard Katy's sharp intake of breath, felt the bite of her fingers as she clutched at his arm. But Blaine was fully aware only of Sid Reece. Everyone else in the room faded to insignificance. He could feel his heart pounding wildly, and he felt a demanding impulse to get to his feet and hurl himself at Sid Reece. But he didn't. He sat where he was, not moving, because that was all he could do.

Then as swiftly as his anger had risen, Sid became calm again. He lowered the gun and dropped the hammer. He looked hard at Blaine and shook his head.

'That's too quick for you, Blaine,' he said. 'You ain't goin' to get off so easy, feller.'

Blaine didn't reply. He was still shaken. It was no joke being so close to a bullet. And having it happen twice in one day was no easier. *Tread careful, brother,* he warned himself, *the next time the reprieve might come after the hammer's fallen.*

'Forget him, Sid,' Matthew said. 'We got some planning to do.'

'Yeah, okay, okay,' Sid mumbled, and there was a sharp edge to his voice. He jammed the gun in his pants and backed away from Blaine.

Ned had found a bottle of whiskey in a cupboard. He uncorked it and set it down on the table. Sid reached for it as soon as he sat down. He tilted it over his lips and drained off a good third. He passed the bottle to Matthew, who took only a short swallow. Ned had similar tastes to Sid, and the bottle was almost empty when he slopped it back on the table. Jubal made no move to touch it. He sat with his huge hands flat on the table, watching his brothers intently.

'They don't serve stuff like that

where I was,' Sid laughed. He belched loudly. 'Man, that worked fast.' He wiped his dripping mouth with the back of his hand. 'All right, Matt, let's hear what you got in mind.'

Matthew pulled off his hat and ran his hands through his thick hair.

'I been figurin' it's time we quit this territory and lit out for somewhere else. For one thing the law and the army are workin' too close together now. It ain't like the old days, even though they were only a short time back. Up to now we've been damn lucky. But what happened to Sid could happen again. And we might not pull off another stunt like we did today.'

'Matt's right,' Ned said. 'We've run our luck pretty thin around here. With the law and army after us, and the whole damn Apache nation on the loose, this chunk of God's earth is goin' to be a mite too chancy. I say we ought to move out. There's a hell of a lot more to this country than Arizona and New Mexico.'

Sid listened without comment. He hung back in his chair, his head tilted forward. There was a hungry look in his eyes. He was watching Katy.

'I thought we might head up toward the Dakotas,' Matt went on. 'Plenty of pickings up that way. Besides, we'd be nearer the Canadian border up there. What you say, Sid?'

Sid nodded slowly. 'I'm easy. Don't make no difference where I light. Long as there's a bottle and a woman in reach.' He was still staring at Katy.

Katy herself stiffened sharply and would have risen had it not been for Blaine's hand on her arm.

Sid reached for the bottle again. He finished off the contents in one swallow. Then he slammed the bottle back on to the table. The bottle fell on its side and rolled off the edge of the table. It bounced, but didn't break when it hit the wooden floor, then rolled gently across the worn planks until it was halted by the heel of Katy's left boot. Sid watched this and smiled. Pushing to his feet, he took a couple of unsteady steps.

'Sid,' Matt said sharply.

'Leave me be,' Sid mumbled hotly. 'You been here long enough. You just lost your chance. Don't spoil mine. Brother.' The last word he almost spat out.

He halted alongside Katy. Grinned. 'C'mon, sis, don't be bashful.' He snaked out an arm, his big hand clamping on to Katy's shoulder, fingers digging in hard.

Forgetting all, Blaine pushed up from the floor. As he rose he swung his clenched right fist at Sid. It caught the outlaw behind the ear. Sid grunted with pain and backed off. He wiped a hand over his ear.

'You bastard!' he yelled, angry and hurt.

He threw himself at Blaine and the two of them smashed into the log wall. A stunning pain spread across Blaine's back as his shoulder was ground against the rough logs. Sid's fist crashed hard against his mouth. Blaine felt his legs giving way. Something slammed into his stomach and he fell to his knees. He stayed there, unable to rise, waves of sickness sweeping over him. He could feel blood running down his back. He waited for the next blow.

Instead, a long way off, he heard Katy's voice.

'Leave him. For God's sake, leave him. You'll kill him. He's been hurt. Can't you see the blood?'

Then Sid's voice. 'Ain't that a shame now. Makes no difference to me. Why should I go easy on him? After what he done to me. Why?'

'Because I ask you to,' Katy said. She was on her feet now, brushing back her hair from her face.

Sid faced her. 'Meaning?'

'You . . . you want me? All right. But on condition nothing happens to Ed.'

The silence that followed was so acute it seemed unnatural. Then Sid let out a great sigh.

'You on the level?'

Katy faced him squarely. 'Do you

think I'd joke about something like this?'

'I guess not. But I don't have to make any bargains. I can take you any time.'

'You could,' Katy said firmly.

Sid grinned. 'But I like the way you do things. You got a deal, sis.'

'Katy, don't do this,' Blaine shouted. He had to shout because he couldn't hear properly. He fell back against the wall again. His eyes were open but all he could see was a swirling red mist with dark shapes moving across his field of vision.

Katy knelt beside him, wiping blood from his lips. His groping hand found hers.

'Katy, *please*.'

'Ed, listen. Understand me, please. There's no other way. Do you think I like doing this? I could let him kill you. But I want you alive, Ed. Do you want to be dead? Is that what you want?'

'Damn it, no. But what kind of bargain is it you're offering? Katy, don't do it for me. Not for me.'

'But it is for you, Ed. Because I love you.' She paused. 'It won't be anything new to me. You know that. You know the kind of life I led working in that saloon. Maybe the gossips back at Fort Clay were right about a saloon-girl not being able to get away from her kind of life. Maybe my running away didn't do any good . . . they say you can't escape your life by running. It always catches up.'

Blaine tried to get up. Pain kept him in its grip, tearing at his nerves. But the mist was fading from his eyes. 'Katy,' he said. Then he realized her hand was gone from his.

Sickness rose in him. He fought against his pain and weakness. But now hard hands held him down, and he felt a gun barrel pushed sharply into his side. His vision had cleared enough for him to look at the grinning face of Ned Reece.

'Sid's going to be busy awhile. And he don't like to be disturbed. You know how it is.'

Somewhere at the back of the cabin a door closed.

★ ★ ★

'So this is where you bunk out,' Sid said.

He shoved Katy into the small room. Pushed the door shut sharply.

The sound of the door closing made Katy's heart leap. She was frightened. More than she'd ever been in her life. Her entire being trembled as she faced Sid. She wanted to run from him, to scream. But she didn't, and she wouldn't. Because on her depended the life of the man she loved. She hoped she would be strong enough to go through with it.

Sid finished his examination of the room. He turned to Katy. She backed away a step before she could check herself. Sid grinned.

'That ain't goin' to 'complish much, sis. This room's too small for them sort of games. Be easier all round if'n you just kept still.'

He moved swiftly then, blocking the way past him, backing her into a corner. His arms encircled her, pulled her hard against him. His mouth sought hers. Despite her promise to him Katy found herself resisting violently.

'Just you fight on, sis,' Sid gasped. 'Ain't nothing like a little fire in a woman to make it worthwhile.'

Slowly his overpowering strength was too much for her.

Katy's struggles lessened and Sid felt her body soften against him. He freed one hand from round her body, used it to pluck open the buttons of her shirt. He jerked the opened garment roughly from her shoulders, gazing greedily at the naked beauty of her breasts. Katy bit back a sob as his hand circled roughly, harshly across the firm flesh.

'Man, oh, man,' Sid said softly.

Muffled, but still loud enough to draw instant reaction, came the sudden boom of a handgun. Once, then again. Followed by a shrill scream that went on and on and on.

'What in hell!'

Sid froze, indecision hard on the heels of surprise. Then just as swiftly he moved into action, pushing Katy aside. He flung open the door, clawing for the gun at his belt.

Voices mingled with the crash of footsteps. Then more gunshots.

But none of this was heard in the small room, at the back of the cabin. Katy Warner, crouched by the side of the bed, buried her face in the sheets and cried. Fully and unashamedly she cried like a child.

Ned was the only one left in the cabin when the rush had carried his brothers outside. The only Reece. His gun, though, covered six men. Six men who would have, if given the chance, killed him with as much thought one gives to killing a fly.

Ned was nervous. It showed. In his face, his actions. He was anxious to find out what had caused the shooting outside. Wondering if his brothers were all right, if any of them had been hurt.

Hoping that they would find it to be some insignificant occurrence. His eyes flickered uneasily from his captives to the open doorway and then back to the men under his gun.

And what of those men who sat before the menace of Ned Reece's gun?

Their bodies were tense, ready to move into violent action should the chance arise. They were six men with one thought, one desire, spurred on by their will to live, to survive. Men born and bred in a land where death was as close as the shirt on a man's back, or as far as the next mountain peak. But men who had no wish to die; for each had his dreams to fulfill, no matter how small, each his own personal mountain to conquer. So they watched and waited for a chance to turn the tables on the men who held the whip hand over them.

Chad Butler was watching Ned very closely. His sharp eyes noticed the momentary jerk that shook Ned's gun hand every minute or so. He guessed

Ned to be a high-strung character. A man who at moments of extreme tension was apt to become jittery, unnerved. It made him a dangerous man, Chad realized. If anybody made a sharp move that was out of order, Ned was liable to start loosing off lead in every direction under the sun. But on the other hand Ned's condition might play him right into a trap of his own creation.

Beside Chad was Ed Blaine. The man was leaning hard against the wall. His face was set, streaked with blood and sweat. Blaine sat motionless, his eyes fixed on some invisible spot between floor and ceiling. Chad nudged him, hoping Ned was too concerned with his own worries to notice. He wasn't sure how Blaine would respond. He knew the soldier was in poor condition. Blaine had been wounded, lost a fair amount of blood, and it was anybody's guess how long it had been since he'd had a decent period of rest. Even his stay at the station had been rough. Blaine was tough, Chad admitted. But just how much could a man take? How much before he gave in?

But Chad had to take a chance. If anything was to be done, it had to be accomplished now. Before the Reeces came back. That gave them how long? A minute, two, three? How long? Chad kicked the thought aside. He nudged Blaine again.

Blaine didn't move. But Chad heard his whispered,

'Ned?'

Chad nodded his head slightly. He silently thanked God for Blaine's alertness. He knew he was asking a lot from the man, but he was confident Blaine would be with him on anything he did. That was why he had chosen Blaine to one of the others.

'Make it good. I'll back you,' Blaine said softly.

Ned's head swung round. His gun followed, settled on Blaine.

'What you sayin', soldier?'

'He wants some water. He's in a bad way,' Chad said.

'Let the bastard thirst,' Ned snapped.

A crackle of gunfire rolled into the room from somewhere outside.

'Easy, gents.' Ned's gun waved back across the line of men. 'Just sit easy.'

'Pity you can't, Reece,' Chad said gently.

'What?'

'You heard me, boy. You look a mite upset. Thinkin' maybe your brothers are gettin' shot up out there? Maybe so if a posse's caught up with you.'

'Quit yappin', mister,' Ned threatened. 'Boys'll be back any minute.'

More gunfire rolled on the hot air.

'Sounds busy out there,' Chad said. 'Wonder how many of your brothers are still standing? Reckon you'll be next?'

'Keep it up, mister, and I'll give you a bellyful.'

Chad managed a faint smile. 'You goin' to chance it? That gun'll make a big noise. If that's a posse out there, a shot'll bring 'em running.' He paused. 'I thought you Reeces were smart.'

Slowly, almost too slowly, Chad's needling began to tell on Ned. A band of sweat streaked his forehead. He paced into the center of the room. The fingers of his gun hand curled and twisted round the butt of his Colt.

'Worried?' Chad asked. So gently, prodding artfully.

'Shut up,' Ned yelled. He spun round on Chad. The finger that lay across the trigger of his Colt was white. Chad pushed in his knife a little more. 'Boy, you look yellow. You sure you ain't gettin' ready to run?'

Two swift strides brought Ned beside Chad. All caution was forgotten, all suspicions cast aside in his anger. Raw, unchecked anger that showed in his flared nostrils, his burning, gleaming eyes.

'Mister, I done heard enough of your crap.' Ned let the hammer down on his Colt as he spoke, swung it at Chad's head.

The blow never landed. Blaine, who had held himself motionless throughout, now came suddenly alive. His left foot snaked out and hooked around Ned's left ankle.

Then Blaine kicked out hard with his right foot. The heel of his boot struck Ned's leg just under the knee. At the same time Blaine yanked with his left leg. Ned gave a shrill cry as pain spread up his leg. Dizziness swept over him as the wrenching pain engulfed his entire limb. It collapsed, pitched him to his knees. His gun spun from his hand as he hit the floor.

Chad gave a whoop of triumph. He shoved up off the floor and yanked Ned Reece upright. It was with a great deal of satisfaction that he drove his fist deep into Ned's stomach, then landed a savage right to the outlaw's jaw.

Ned pitched to the floor and lay moaning softly. Chad picked up Ned's fallen gun, reversed it and slammed the butt down across the back of Ned's skull.

'Don't want him yellin' his fool head off,' he said. He crossed over to the window and peered out. 'Hell, they're heading back. Looks like one of them is hurt. They're carryin' him. That kid. Hoby.'

He turned from the window and joined the others.

They were grouped round the oak chest that held the confiscated guns. Since the last attempt at escape had meant smashing the lock, the chest was no problem.

Throwing open the lid Blaine passed out weapons. He kept a .44 caliber Remington revolver for himself.

'Let's try and take them without shooting,' Blaine said. 'It'll be a hell of a mess if we all start blasting away in here.'

Tom Peak and Harvy Martin dragged the unconscious Ned Reece out of sight. Then along with Chad and Ham and Sam Loren they positioned themselves clear of the window and door. Blaine stood behind the half-open door, the gun in his hand cocked and ready.

They hadn't long to wait. Boots pounded the earth outside, then Sid Reece burst into the room.

'Ned, it's Hoby. Got a goddamn kni . . . ' His voice trailed off as he realized Ned wasn't in sight. He raised his gun, spun on his heel as he searched the room with angry eyes.

Blaine stepped out from behind the door. In one swift movement he laid the barrel of his revolver across Sid's head. Sid grunted and staggered drunkenly. Blaine hit him again and Sid dropped to the floor. Blaine kicked the gun out of Sid's fingers. Then he stepped away from the door as footsteps sounded just outside.

Matthew and Jubal came in. They carried Hoby between them, and were too surprised by the appearance of their captives, now holding the guns, to be able to offer resistance.

Blaine kicked the door shut. He glanced at Hoby. The younger Reece was unconscious now. The knife was still buried in his chest. Blood soaked his shirt down to his waist.

'Apache?' Blaine asked.

Matthew nodded. 'Bastard got away too.'

'Put him on the table,' Blaine said.

He remembered to remove Matthew's Colt from his holster.

Chad cleared the table with a sweep of his arm. Hoby was laid gently across the table by his brothers.

'Let me see him,' Chad said. Matthew Reece stepped aside without a word.

'Watch them,' Blaine said to Tom Peak. The deputy nodded.

Blaine pushed through the curtained door into the rear of the cabin. At the moment he had one thought only in his mind. One objective. Find Katy. One hope. That she would be unharmed. And making a promise that if she were harmed in any way he would kill Sid Reece with his bare hands.

He reached the first bedroom and kicked open the door. The room was empty.

'Katy!' he shouted. His heart began to pound. And his stomach began to coil and twist with a mixture of fear and anxiety. 'Katy.'

'Ed.' Her voice sounded small and lost after the sound of his own frantic call. She leaned against the door frame of the next room, holding out one hand toward him.

Blaine took three steps and caught her as she fell into his arms. She clung to him as though clinging to life itself, and her body was shaken by great unchecked sobs. He raised a hand and stroked the tumbling mass of her hair, but apart from that he left her alone, content to hold her close.

Gradually she calmed down. Her body became still as she took control. Slowly she raised her head. Her face was wet with tears, her eyes red-rimmed. But she had a smile for him as their eyes met.

'Did he . . . ?' Blaine asked.

Katy shook her head. 'Not that he didn't want to. I must look a sight,' she said. She tried to sound unconcerned, but there was a tone to her voice, a faint quiver that she could not conceal.

'You look fine,' Blaine said, and he meant it. He bent his head and kissed her. 'Hell of a woman. How did I ever get mixed up with you? Tell me.'

Katy laughed. It came bubbling through her tears. Unchecked and completely spontaneous. And for a moment they were in a place far removed from Butler's Station.

But it was an illusion that lasted only a moment and was wiped away when Katy asked, 'Ed, what was all that shooting about? Was anyone hurt?'

He told her all that had taken place, saw her face pale as he mentioned the Apache, heard her ask, 'What can we do, Ed?'

Blaine rubbed his aching, nagging shoulder. He was feeling weak again.

'Damned if I know,' he said. 'If it was an Apache the Reeces saw, we may be in worse trouble than we are now. Apaches seldom travel alone. I'll bet any odds that one was at scout for a larger group. If he gets back to them we'll find ourselves with a raiding party to deal with.'

'Then wouldn't it be best if we left here? Before they come?'

'I don't think so. We're a long way from anyone who could help us. Second, we don't know how many Apaches we may be up against. Or where they are. If we go riding off we might land right in the middle of them. Out in the open we wouldn't stand much of a chance. If we stay here and wait it out, I reckon we might pull through.'

One way or another, Blaine decided, *hell is going to start popping very shortly.*

18

Torrio fell from his pony's back into Chana's arms. The Apache lowered his companion to the ground as gently as a baby. The rest of his warriors began to gather round but Chana cleared them away with a sharp command.

He turned back to Torrio with a water-skin in his hands, but Torrio pushed it aside.

'Keep it for those who still live. It is too late for me, my brother,' he whispered. Blood flecked his lips.

'I will not hear such talk,' Chana said. 'Who did this to you? The whites at the station?'

Torrio nodded. His eyes flickered, closed, then opened again.

'I failed you, Chana. You were right. My time is over. I am too old for war.'

He began to cough violently, and blood spilled from his mouth, streaking his chin and throat.

'Rest quietly. You will soon be strong and well again,' Chana said. But as he spoke he knew Torrio would fight no more, would never again ride the secret trails only the Apache knew.

Torrio reached up and clasped one of Chana's hands in his own.

'Think of me, Chana. Pray that the spirits will accept me.' He coughed again, choked as blood filled his throat.

His grip on Chana's hand relaxed. When Chana lowered his eyes to him, Torrio was dead.

For a long time Chana sat beside his friend, staring down into the dead face and recalling the past years they had spent together. From the time they were mere children playing naked in the dust, up to the time of their initiation into manhood and the ways of their tribe, they had been together. In peace and in war, they had been like one. Chana the born leader, the man of action. Torrio the thinker, the advisor. Different in many ways, but still so alike.

But now all that was ended. Chana was alone. He felt as though part of him had died with Torrio.

The whites had killed Torrio. They would pay. Very dearly. The blood of the *Pinda Lickoyi* would darken the earth and the sky would echo the sound of their screams. Chana hoped he could take some of them alive. For his thoughts now were for vengeance. For Torrio. This day the whites would feel the full fury of the Apache.

Chana rose. He turned to his waiting warriors.

'We take the station,' he said. 'They have taken the life of our brother. Fight well, my warriors, and we shall destroy this white man's place called Butler's Station.'

Chana took the blanket from Torrio's pony and covered his friend's body. Then he mounted his own pony and waited until his warriors were mounted.

'Are you ready, my warriors?' he challenged.

'*Aiii, Chana, we are ready,*' came the shouted reply.

Chana swept his arm up and kicked his pony into swift movement. Shrill whoops and yells rent the hot air as the rest of the Apaches followed him. The thunder of their ponies' hoofs rolled about in the air as dust boiled up in the wake of the galloping group. They burst out of the clump of rocks and streamed across the naked plain, heading for Butler's Station.

★　★　★

'I don't know if he'll live. It's out of my hands now,' Chad Butler said. He picked up a damp cloth and began to wipe blood from his fingers.

Matthew Reece stared at the heavy-bladed knife in his hand. Chad had just removed it from Hoby's chest. Now, Hoby lay on the couch, a blanket over him. He was still unconscious, and his breathing was harsh and irregular. His face was pale, bloodless, shiny with sweat.

Blaine sat at Katy's side across the

room from the group around Hoby Reece. Sam Loren straddled a chair in front of Blaine. His damaged arm was in a sling that Katy had fashioned for him, and he held a cup of steaming black coffee in his good hand.

'And I'll stake my life they was 'Pache we spotted on our way in,' he was saying.

'That about confirms it then,' Blaine said.

'It sure puts us in a spot,' Loren observed. 'But if it comes to a fight, I'm with you on sticking it out here. We try to make a run for it we wouldn't get half a mile.'

'If we organize properly, I reckon we'll be able to make a good fight,' Blaine said. 'We don't lack for guns or ammunition. And with eleven of us we should be able to stand off a fair amount of Apaches.'

'*Eleven?*' Loren looked at him sharply. 'You mean you'd give guns to them Reeces? After we just took 'em away from them?'

'If the Apaches hit us we're going to need every gun firing. The Reeces are just as much involved as we are. The Apaches are going to be shooting at them too. No matter what they've done, they have the right to protect themselves. We can't deny them that right. But until we're sure one way or another, we keep the guns, and the Reeces do as we tell them.'

Loren nodded. 'Yeah. I guess that sounds all right, Blaine.'

Tom Peak crossed over to Blaine. He carried his shotgun cradled in his right arm. 'Blaine, you and Loren know this country. What chances are there for a man to get through for help?'

'If he goes easy and doesn't take chances, pretty good. Trouble is the nearest army post is Fort Kane. It's a small settlement on the Gila River. There's a small garrison there. But it's three days' ride from here.'

'I know that place,' Loren said. 'But there's a heap of rough country before you reach it.'

Peak sighed. 'Well, I reckon someone ought to go. We need some help one way or another.'

'You got anybody in mind?' Blaine asked.

'I already got him. Ham Butler. I talked to him. He says if someone tells him which way to go he'll give it a try.'

'I reckon Sam and me can draw him a rough map,' Blaine said. 'Get him over here.'

Peak went to get Ham. After a search Katy found paper and pencil for Blaine. With Sam Loren's help, Blaine sketched a route-map, noting down various landmarks that would help Ham on his journey.

'You sure you want to go?' Blaine asked when Ham joined them.

Ham nodded. His face was still sore, covered with nasty blue-black bruises. He caught sight of Katy watching him. He wouldn't look at her. He felt a deep sense of shame come over him. His attitude toward her had been wrong. He knew this now. He saw how shallow and childish his actions had been. Katy was a proud woman. But today she had discarded her pride to save the man she loved from being hurt, perhaps killed. She had been right when she had rejected his advances and told him to wait until he was a man. That was something he had yet to become. In a way Ham's offer to go for help was an effort to redeem himself in Katy's eyes. And also to prove to himself that he was man enough to live up to all his daydreaming. Though he didn't know it, Ham was taking his first step toward growing up.

Blaine handed the map to Ham and told him what to do when he got to Fort Kane. 'Do most of your travelling by dark. It's safer. And it won't tire the horse or you so much. Just think before you do anything and don't take chances.'

'Yes, sir.'

Chad came across, his face lined with worry. He looked at his son as though seeing him for the first time. 'Ham, you want to go?'

'Yes, Pa. I do. Anyhow, I know the

country around here. And I got a map.'

'You feel fit to ride?'

'I reckon so,' Ham said.

Chad rubbed his chin. He was concerned. And it showed.

'He'll be all right, Chad,' Blaine said. 'I don't think he'll have much trouble. From the way things look the Apaches will be coming in from the east. Ham's heading north-west. That's clear away. If he takes off up the creek for a few miles, then heads across country he'll be well clear by the time it gets dark. Then he can make good time until dawn.'

'If'n the boy can get clear, why can't the rest of us?'

Blaine glanced sharply up at the speaker. It was Sid Reece. There was a raw bruise over his left eye where Blaine had hit him.

'Because one boy doesn't make as much noise as a dozen people. Or attract as much attention. I thought you were smart, Reece. You at least should have figured that much out.'

Sid turned away in disgust, unable to mask his feelings for Blaine.

When Ham had collected a sack of supplies and a rifle, he and his father slipped out the back door of the cabin and made their cautious way to the barn. After almost twenty minutes Chad came back into the cabin. He crossed over to Blaine.

'He's away. Damned if I wasn't more worried than he was. Must admit I'm proud of that boy. Never thought he had it in him.'

'Funny what a situation like this can do to a man. It can bring out his best. Or his worst.'

'What do we do now?' Chad asked. He was sweating heavily.

'We wait. And hope that a certain bunch of Apaches decide they don't want a fight with anyone.'

'You think maybe they won't bother?' Chad questioned hopefully.

Blaine shook his head. 'I doubt it. Just at the present time every Apache in the country is bent on one thing. To try and kill as many whites as possible before they kill him. And it isn't very often they pass up an opportunity to do just that.' He shook his head slowly. 'I reckon we're in for it. Anytime.'

From over by the window Harvy Martin said, 'Anytime is right now.'

They crossed to the window, looked out.

Beyond the corral, and well out of rifle range, amid swirling dust, a bunch of Apache warriors sat motionless on their ponies. Blaine counted well over a dozen of them. They wore full paint markings on their stonily impassive faces. They all carried rifles, and in addition a number of them had bows and long war lances.

'Oh my God,' Tom Peak said softly. He had encountered Apaches before, knew how they fought and had seen the results of their savage ways.

'Man, we are right in the middle,' Sam Loren said. He glanced at the Reeces. 'You boys like fighting. Well, you'll get your bellyful now.'

Matthew joined them at the window.

It was Sid again who asked, 'So now we sit here and wait for them to attack?'

'Isn't it enough?' Blaine said.

'Blaine, you going to let us have guns?' Matthew asked.

'If it does come to a fight you'll be able to defend yourselves. But not until we know one way or the other.'

Blaine looked out at the Apaches again. They had dismounted and were squatting in a group on the ground.

All save one who stood apart, facing the station, his arms folded across his chest.

'And I don't think we'll have long to wait to find out which way it is.'

★ ★ ★

Night came and drew a dark cape across the land. The sun sank slowly, almost as if reluctant to go, leaving its kingdom to the hosts of night. It vanished in a final blaze of red glory. The stars appeared in the vast dark sky and threw their cold light on to the still land. With the darkness came a sharp chill as the ground gave up the warmth it had hoarded during the day.

Beyond Butler's Station a ring of small fires made glowing holes in the darkness. Around them sat Chana's warriors. They waited. And as they waited they ate and talked and readied their weapons.

Chana himself sat alone, a blanket around his broad shoulders. He sat facing the station. Chana's eyes gleamed in the reflected firelight. Anger was in his heart as he saw light appear in the window of the distant cabin. He could imagine the whites moving around inside their building.

Talking, eating, alive while Torrio lay cold and unmoving beneath a thin blanket. But this would be changed, Chana promised.

With a decisive movement Chana threw off his blanket. He rose and walked toward his warriors.

★   ★   ★

Some kind of defense plan had been called for in case the Apaches attempted a night attack. Blaine sent Tom Peak and Harvy Martin into the rear of the cabin. There were no side windows in the building; only the one in the front and four small ones at the back. The ground around the cabin was flat and open for a good distance too, so it was not going to be easy for the Apaches to effect a sneak attack. The darkness would help them; but light from the window threw a wide patch that spread across the front of the cabin. Anyone keeping close watch by the window stood a good chance of spotting any movement in the area.

All weapons in the cabin were checked and fully loaded. Chad produced a surprisingly large amount of ammunition.

'Courtesy of the stage-line,' he said. 'Since the Apache trouble came up, all stations have been supplied with extra rifles and ammunition. Never thought I'd ever need to use it.'

Blaine made a final check. He

realized there was nothing more they could do. Once again all they could do was wait.

It touched everybody. He glanced across the room to where Katy was kneeling before the fireplace, feeding logs into the steady blaze she had going. Waiting had almost lost her for him. Waiting instead of marrying her straight off. Too much waiting he decided tiredly. Blaine crossed over and sank into a chair against the wall. His eyes felt heavy. He wanted to sleep. He needed to. If he was to be alert when trouble came he needed to relax for a while.

There was only waiting now, so he could afford to rest.

Chad and Sam Loren were watching the Reeces. He could leave them to it. Neither of them was the sort to stand for any messing about. And anyhow he didn't think the Reeces were going to try anything. Not with Hoby in his condition. Nor with a bunch of Apaches just outside. At this time they all needed each other. And even the Reeces were smart enough to realize that fact.

Blaine let his weary body relax. He felt the tension drain from him. He closed his eyes, tried again to ignore the pain from his shoulder. He was tired. So tired. It had been a long time since he had been so weary. Years in fact.

His tired, jumbled mind returned him to a time in his life he had managed to forget. But memories came flooding back, and he was too weary, too confused to fight them off. They filled his head, seemed to parade before his eyes like a nightmare . . .

It was 1863. September. At a place called Chickamauga.

There were hundreds of men. In uniform. And he was there too. Private Edwin Oliver Blaine. He'd been young and scared and tired. But there was no rest. The only men lying down were either dead or dying. No rest. Just fight to stay alive. Surrounded by death and noise and confusion.

No rest. Only advance with the rest of the Union troops. It had gone on for two days. Men had fallen like so many dead leaves. And as one man fell another stepped into his place. Blaine had been one of those who managed to keep going through it all, though he never knew what it was that kept him going. He moved like a man in a dream, his legs heavy, his movements sluggish. Barely able to keep his eyes open. But knowing he must, he had to. If he wished to stay alive. And he did. Firing and reloading, advancing, retreating. With only one purpose, one thought, to kill the enemy before he killed you. Kill Rebs. Kill, destroy. It became a madness that controlled a man. Took him over until he was merely the thing that carried and aimed and fired the rifle. Took him over so he became unaware of the bloody slaughter around him. Unaware of the roar of guns, the swirling smoke, the screams of wounded men. A stumbling, groping being who fought on blindly, paying no attention to the pleading cries for help from ragged, smashed creatures that had once been men. And it went on and on. Until that moment when his world vanished in a blinding, screaming flash of light and sound. He had the momentary feeling he was far from the death and noise, then a great wave of pain swept over him and he felt no more, heard nothing more. But in that instant before consciousness left him, he remembered thinking, *Now I can sleep . . .*

'*Blaine. Blaine.* Wake up, man.'

He opened his eyes. He knew what he would see. The weary face of the army doctor who would tell him how lucky he was not to have been killed by that shell burst, that he'd be all right in a few weeks. Those weeks had stretched into ten long months, with a lot of pain . . .

Blaine jerked his eyes fully open. Chad Butler was shaking him gently.

'How long have I been asleep?'

'About five hours,' Chad grinned.

'Hell, you should have woken me.'

'No need. Till now.'

Blaine straightened. 'Trouble?'

Chad nodded. 'We spotted movement out by the corral.'

Blaine followed him to where Matthew Reece crouched by the window. He indicated the north end of the corral.

'Wouldn't swear but I'd say it was a man. If the damn moon would show, it'd make our chances that much more even.'

Blaine turned from the window as Katy brought him a cup of coffee. The hot, black liquid woke him to full alertness. He was grateful for the few hours of sleep, although he was stiff, his shoulder tight and throbbing.

'See anything else?' Blaine asked.

Matthew shook his head. He turned to speak to Blaine. As he did the glass in the window exploded inward.

Matthew spun away from the window as shattered shards of glass burst across the room. And something hissed a swift path through the air, striking the far wall with a solid chunk.

It was an Apache arrow. Decorated

with the signs of war.

In the silence that followed, so acute it was painful, no one moved.

Then from outside, somewhere in the darkness, came a long, high howl of defiance. It echoed and spun around the cabin, and if it did nothing else, it at least told the occupants what lay ahead.

Blaine caught Matthew Reece watching him. Matthew's face was streaked with blood from a number of glass cuts.

'How about those guns now?' he asked.

Blaine glanced at the other Reeces. At Sid, eyes gleaming with anticipation, a half-smile playing across his lips. At Ned who hadn't yet taken his eyes from the window. And Jubal. Big and slow, but waiting patiently for Matthew's orders.

Then back to Matthew Reece. Tough, ruthless; but with cold clear logic. A man who knew which way the wind blew and how to use it to his own advantage.

Blaine felt Katy standing beside him

and was aware of the responsibility he had to her, and the others who were involved in the decision he had to make. There was so much to decide, he knew, but so little time.

'*Well?*' Matthew asked again.

Blaine raised his eyes to meet Matthew's gaze. 'Chad,' he said, 'break out rifles and ammunition.'

19

Matthew Reece sat on a straight-backed chair alongside the couch where Hoby lay. It was well after midnight, and a sharp chill had crept into the cabin. A couple of hours back they had used up the last of the logs. Now, the fire had died to a pile of glowing ashes. The only light in the room was provided by two oil lamps which cast long, deep shadows across the walls and floor.

Across the shadowed room Matthew could see Ed Blaine sitting motionless in the window's pale outline, a rifle in his hands. For some reason, and despite what had happened between them, Matthew Reece silently admitted a tolerant respect for Blaine. There was something about the man that intrigued Matthew in this moment of calm. Was it, he asked himself, the deep, earnest faith that Blaine had in his beliefs about the country and the people who were trying to make something out of nothing? Or was it the stubborn, dogged way he kept coming right back no matter what the odds? And after some thought Matthew decided that the enigma of Ed Blaine was an amalgam of both. Blaine simply believed in his way, and would let nothing deter him from that way. But it was the calm, rock-steady way he went about things. Matthew shook his head slowly, and found himself hoping it would never come to the point of having to kill Blaine. He realized with some surprise he saw in the man a lot of what he himself would liked to have been.

In the darkest corner of the room Sid Reece squatted on his heels, his rifle across his knees. Sid was taking some time out to do some hard thinking of his own.

Sid's thoughts were mainly running along the lines of how he could get himself out of his present position. It was not to Sid's liking. He'd just spent three months in a stinking prison cell. And now, after a short moment of freedom, here he was a damned prisoner again.

From where he squatted Sid could see Ed Blaine beside the window. Raising his rifle Sid squinted along the barrel. So damned easy. Just one quick pull of the trigger and there would be one less bastard in the world. His mind still on the same vicious level, Sid swung the muzzle around until it centered on Matthew's broad back. *And you, brother, who got me out of the pan, right into the goddamn fire.* There was no gratitude in Sid for what his brother had done, only cold, raw anger and thoughts of violence because he was still a captive.

Sid tilted the rifle at the floor. *Damn 'em all,* he swore savagely. *I don't need 'em, any of 'em. It's time ol' Sid kicked free from the family corral. I ain't aimin' to let no stinkin' 'Pache take me. I got me some livin' to do yet. First chance I get, I'm headin' out, fast and wide.*

He let his gaze rove around the room until he spotted the motionless figure of the woman, a blanket-wrapped form at Blaine's feet. Sid grinned in the darkness. Now there was a shame, him and her being interrupted earlier.

Could have been right enjoyable. But that stupid kid Hoby had to go and tangle with that Apache. Seemed a pity a woman like that being wasted on a no 'count 'Pache buck who wouldn't even realize what he'd got hold of. Maybe, just maybe, when ol' Sid headed for the High Lonesome he wouldn't be alone. Might be tricky, but hell, it'd be worth it.

'Ed. Ed.'

Katy's low voice reached Blaine from the shadows at his feet. He didn't take his eyes from the window. 'I hear you.'

'You want a boy or a girl?'

Blaine let the question sink in. It was so unexpected he was silenced for a moment.

'God, we're not even married yet, woman.'

199

'I know. But tell me anyhow.'

Blaine laughed softly. 'Damned if I'll ever understand a woman. Of all the times to ask . . . '

'Stop evading the question.'

'Well . . . I reckon a boy. A son,' Blaine said. And liked the sound it had.

Katy sighed, pleased. 'So would I,' she said.

Chad Butler was thinking about a son. His son. Ham.

Worry gnawed his insides, mingled with the pulsing pride of a man who suddenly realizes his son, his child, has become a man. He knew that things would be better when Ham got back. If he got back, doubt said. *Ahh, he'll get back.* Ham would do all right. Hell, he was a Butler, wasn't he?

★ ★ ★

Two hours before dawn the Apaches made their first move against the station.

While the main band kept up a

200

deadly, continuous fire that kept the occupants of the cabin under cover, four braves, led by Chana himself, made a circuitous approach to the barn. Once inside they freed and stampeded all the horses. They then set fire to the barn and vanished into the night under cover of the smoke.

The firing ceased as swiftly as it had started. Silence fell again, broken only by the hungry roar of the burning barn.

The savage outburst of gunfire caused only structural damage inside the cabin. The closest to a casualty was Chad Butler who caught a flying splinter of wood across his right cheek.

The window was completely stripped of its frame and glass now. And the far wall, directly opposite from the window, was pockmarked deeply. Raw, white wood-splinters littered the floor, along with chunks of adobe and shattered glass.

Pinned down by the withering fire from the Apaches' guns the cabin's defenders were forced to sit and listen in helpless fury while the Apaches ran off their horses. And then they saw the blackness of night glow red as the barn became a blazing pyre.

They sat and waited; no more were they able to do.

No word was spoken. They rested as much as possible, because they knew now that dawn would bring the full fury of the Apaches' attack.

20

The beginning of a new day. The advancing light paled the blackness of night, and cleared the way for the sweeping blue curves of the clean, open sky. Warmth flooded across the cold earth, and the final shadows of night fled from the searching fingers of the sun. And in that brief period when time seemed to slow and pause momentarily, silence was predominant.

The Apaches came with the dawn.

The empty quiet was shattered as the brown warriors erupted out of nowhere, it seemed to the defenders of Butler's Station. Unshod hoofs pounded the raw earth in a staccato rhythm; the air was alive with shrill yells and shrieks as the Apaches drove their sturdy ponies in a dead run at the cabin.

'*Here they come!*'

Sam Loren's yell brought swift

action. Matthew and Sid joined him at the window. Blaine and Chad took up their positions at the barricaded front door; they had pulled a heavy oak chest-of-drawers across the open door space.

A little to one side of the door, along the front wall, they had dragged Hoby Reece's couch. Once, during the night, Hoby had opened his eyes for a few minutes. Then he had lapsed into unconsciousness again. Now he was pale and still, his breathing shallow and ragged, and every now and then there was a dry, rasping rattle in his throat.

Katy divided her attention between watching Hoby and keeping all the spare guns loaded and ready.

The first line of Apaches reached the cabin. They swept past, firing wildly, and circled the cabin, drawing fire from the waiting guns there, then pounded out of range again in preparation for another run.

Rifles crackled viciously as the mounted warriors reached the cabin front. Heavy slugs plowed into the log walls, a few found their way through the window and door, but no one was hit.

A volley of firing from the cabin sent swift slugs after the retreating Apaches. Blaine saw one Apache tilt drunkenly as his shoulder became spattered with red. The Apache's pony faltered, then found its step and bore its rider out of range.

From the cabin the defenders were able to see the Apaches reform. They circled into a milling group, dust boiling up beneath the stamping hoofs of their wiry ponies.

'They're testing us out,' Blaine said. 'Trying to estimate how many guns we've got.'

'Let 'em come,' Sid muttered darkly. He was in a surly mood. Angry at being trapped, at having to fight for his life.

A distant yell brought their attention back to the immediate danger. The Apaches were in motion again, sweeping in a deadly curve toward the cabin.

Blaine leveled his rifle and sighted down the barrel. He waited until his target was big in his sights before he squeezed the trigger gently. His rifle spat flame and smoke. He saw the Apache throw his arms high as the slug took him dead-center in the chest. Then the buck was gone from his pony's back, lost beneath the pounding hoofs of the other ponies.

Beside Blaine, Chad Butler was emptying his rifle with the speed of a Gatling gun. One Apache was knocked from his mount and another caught a slug in the leg before Chad's gun clicked empty.

At the window Matthew Reece fired shell after shell with methodical precision. Sam Loren drove off each shot as though it was his last. Sid however blazed away wildly, cursing profanely all the while. He made a lot of noise, but achieved little else.

Then the Apaches rounded the cabin and the firing took up at the rear. Moments later they swept into view again and streamed out beyond the corral to count their losses and regroup.

Taking advantage of the pause, Katy passed out fresh ammunition.

Harvy Martin burst into the room and crouched beside Blaine.

'How you doing?' Blaine asked.

Martin shrugged. 'We got one, marked a couple of others.'

Blaine nodded. 'Two here,' he said, glancing out at the open yard. 'And at least four wounded. They're not going to like that. It's going to make them just that much wilder. And a hell of a lot smarter.'

'Wait till they belly down in the dirt and start crawlin' in on you. Won't see 'em till they shove a gun butt in your teeth.' Sam Loren thumbed brass-cased shells into his rifle as he spoke.

Blaine glanced out beyond the corral. The Apaches had dismounted and were squatting in a tight group. What the hell were the bastards cooking up? Blaine wondered.

'Tell them to keep wide-eyed back there. I reckon what Sam said is right,' he told Martin.

The deputy nodded and turned away.

Matthew Reece left the window and crossed over to where Hoby lay. Concern marked his face deeply.

'He's still the same,' Katy told him. And thought this was a different side to the Matthew Reece she had come to know in a short, violent time.

'I'm obliged for your kindness,' Matthew said. Then after a pause he added, 'Ma'am,' and returned to his position by the window without another word.

The Apaches made no more attacks. They squatted in the dust and watched the cabin. And those in the cabin returned their gaze.

As the sun rose, so did the temperature. Inside the cabin the air became thick and stifling. Sweat formed with the slightest movement, and was dried by the very heat that had caused it. The skin became dry and irritated, the eyes stung and ached with staring out across the sun-bright land. And with the heat and discomfort, the waiting brought tension; rubbing the nerve ends raw, until a person was jumpy, ready to lash out at anything and anyone.

Blaine noticed these afflictions in himself as well as in the others. And he knew that this was what the Apaches were hoping would happen. It was part of the Apache way of fighting. Endowed with endless patience, the Apache would sit it out, waiting for the strain to break his enemy so that he would be an easy victim.

There was nothing much to do about it either, Blaine saw. They were committed to this fight now. They had to wait for the Apache to bring it to them, for they were in no position to carry it to the Apache. It came down to one single statement of fact. They had to fight the Apache if they wanted to live. Fight until they won. Or lost. Or until help . . . if any . . . arrived. Whichever way you tossed it around, Blaine mused, it always landed dark side uppermost.

Sid Reece waited until Sam Loren

moved down to talk with Blaine.

'Matt, ain't there no way we can get the hell out of this?'

Matthew's smile was cold, almost bleak. 'Only with this,' he said, nudging his rifle.

Sid made an impatient gesture. 'Hell, we done enough tradin' with the 'Paches. Maybe we could talk us out.'

'You want to try? Sid, since you been in jail things have changed a heap. All hell's broke loose. Every damn Apache has put on paint, and every white is dead meat. This time they mean to fight it right down to the last man. Our having traded with them ain't worth a dud cartridge. You remember Jason Poole? Feller who used to run guns up around Mescalero country? Seems a bunch of 'Paches got hold of him and his two partners. I seen what was left of them, Sid, and it made my stomach crawl. So I'd forget any ideas about a pow-wow. You wouldn't get any nearer than the closest rifle slug.'

Sid turned away, scowling darkly. *So*

that's it. Sid swore silently. Then decided he was for getting out the moment he saw a crack in the door.

★   ★   ★

One by one the Apaches began to move, fanning out in a wide semicircle, then flopping out of sight in the dust.

The land beyond the corral appeared empty, save for the bunch of ponies. Nothing moved; nothing in sight.

But the ground crawled with stocky, lithe brown figures that glided unseen, like phantom shadows, toward Butler's Station.

21

The first indication of a fresh attack came when Tom Peak slipped through from the back.

'Thought you'd want to know,' he told Blaine. 'We've spotted half a dozen bucks in the brush along the creek.'

Blaine nodded. 'I sort of expected something like this when they left their ponies and started out on foot. By now they'll be all around us. You better get on back, Tom. And keep on the watch. When they come it'll be fast and hard. We've already hurt 'em, and Apaches don't like it when a fight goes against them. Makes them all the more determined to win.'

Five minutes later a burst of gunfire sounded from the rear of the cabin. Glass shattered and voices rose amid the roar of guns.

'They'll be coming our way any

time,' Blaine warned.

The Apaches swept up from the ground just beyond the corral. They simply appeared from the dust; agile, leaping figures, with flame-spouting rifles in their hands. The air was shrill with their chilling screams.

Blaine ducked as a hail of slugs tore raw slivers of wood from the door frame. Then he swung his rifle through the gap and began triggering off shot after shot at the charging Apaches.

Two bucks went down beneath the concentrated gunfire from the cabin. Another was downed by a slug from Sid Reece's gun, but crawled out of range like a crippled spider running for cover.

Matthew Reece swung away from the window and began to thumb fresh shells into his empty rifle. Moments later Sam Loren emptied his own weapon, and he too turned away from the window.

One Apache managed to reach the cabin despite the devastating rifle fire. Without hesitation he bellied up to the window and swung his rifle butt at Sid Reece. The butt smacked solidly across Sid's skull, spinning him away from the window. The Apache's rifle turned muzzle-first at Sam Loren and the Apache pumped three shots at Loren's back. The range was no more than three feet, and the heavy slugs ripped through the stage driver's body, smashing flesh and bone before they tore jagged holes in his chest on the way out.

The Apache turned his rifle on Matthew Reece. But Matthew was already facing about, his own rifle slicing up from hip level. Matthew triggered off and kept firing until the Apache spun away from the window. As the Apache fell away, Matthew planted himself at the window again.

Katy, by then, was kneeling beside Sam Loren. Gently she turned him on to his back. Her face paled and she felt her stomach tighten as she saw the huge, red-raw wounds in Loren's chest. His entire front was a mass of glistening blood. The man raised his eyes to her face. Beneath his beard his lips formed a smile.

'Don't fret none, child, I don't feel a thing,' he said softly. Then a terrible choking cough filled his throat. Blood bubbled thickly from his mouth as his head rolled slackly.

As Katy moved away from Loren's body she saw Sid Reece sitting up near the wall. He wore a raw bruise across his forehead.

'Never mind the dead,' he snapped. 'Get me something for this.'

Katy felt her anger rise. 'Go to hell,' she told him bitterly, and went back to where Hoby lay. She could feel Sid's eyes on her all the way, but she paid no mind.

Nevertheless, she warned herself to watch out for Sid Reece. He was the worst kind to have for an enemy. Katy couldn't hold back a moment of fear as she pondered on the thought.

The attack held for a while longer; then the Apaches fell back, taking their wounded with them. The firing slackened, finally fading out. In the uneasy calm, as the last echo drifted away, both sides estimated their losses.

Inside the cabin a blue haze of gunsmoke drifted aimlessly to the ceiling.

Blaine covered Sam Loren with a blanket.

'Poor Sam,' Chad said softly, mostly to himself. 'I known him nigh on ten years. First met up with him when he was scouting for the army.'

Blaine wandered through into the back. He checked each man in turn. Out of the four only Harvy Martin had suffered any damage; a rifle slug had taken a chunk of flesh from his right upper arm. Martin had already bound a crude bandage around it.

'We downed two and clipped a couple of others,' Tom Peak told Blaine.

'Don't slack up any just because they've stopped shooting,' Blaine said. 'It don't mean a thing. They're still out there, waiting for another run at us.'

He drifted back into the living room. Matthew and Chad were at their positions. Katy was reloading empty rifles. Sid Reece squatted against the front wall, ignoring everything and everyone.

Blaine joined Katy and watched her for a moment. She raised her head and smiled tiredly.

'You all right?' he asked.

'Yes. But you're not, Ed. You look so tired. And I'm sure that shoulder must be hurting.'

'Not too bad now. Hardly had time to notice it. Bit stiff, but I'll live. I happen to have a good nurse.'

Katy's face sobered as she raised her eyes past Blaine's shoulder and rested on Hoby Reece.

'I wish there was something we could do for him, Ed. For all his toughness and bravado, he's only a boy. He shouldn't die like this.'

'Katy, we've done all we can. When someone's hurt as bad as he is, there's not very much that can be done for them. Agreed, it's not pleasant, but that's the way it is.'

Katy nodded, understanding his words, but her face showed she still felt the same way about it.

★　★　★

Chana crouched in the dust and stared with cold, angry eyes at the remaining twelve warriors of the band. Eight of his finest fighters lay still and silent in the dust of Butler's Station. The Apache leader was outraged that in such a short time his force had been whittled down by a handful of whites. It angered and shamed him. There was no turning away now, no retreat. To quit a fight at this point would bring only dishonor upon Chana and his warriors. This insult to the Apache had to be righted, this Chana knew, before he could hold up his head among his people.

Chana rose and strode into the center of his grouped warriors.

'Hear me, my brothers. I, Chana,

make this vow, upon the memory of my father, Mandano. I will destroy this place of Butler's Station and all who are there. This I vow, and hold all here to bear witness.'

Chana turned and faced the station.

'I shall destroy them,' he said, 'or die, for I will not give in to the *Pinda Lickoyi*. Do you fight with me, brothers?'

A full-throated shout swelled up from the assembled Apaches.

Chana swept up his arm and led his warriors forward once more.

The attack lost Chana one more warrior and gained him nothing. The Apaches withdrew after half an hour of vicious sniping.

It was mid-afternoon. Chana decided that any more rush attacks would only cut down his depleted force even more. The whites were in too good a position. There was only one way for Chana now. And he employed it. He spread out his warriors around the cabin . . . and began to wait.

22

The mid-afternoon attack was the last one that day. Though the Apaches had never gotten close enough to see the cabin's defenders, they inflicted some injury. When they withdrew the Apaches left behind one of their own dead. And the attack marked up a fatality among the defenders of Butler's Station.

Ned Reece, his rifle still clutched in his hands, lay sprawled across the rough planks in one of the back bedrooms. Just above his right eye was a round black hole where a rifle slug had penetrated his flesh on its unswerving path to his brain before blowing out the back of his skull. Jubal Reece carried Ned into the front room and gently laid him alongside the blanket-covered body of Sam Loren.

Matthew knelt beside his dead brother, staring down into the still, pale, bloody face. He lowered his head so no one would see the moistness in his eyes. *It always hits hard*, he realized coldly, *when you lose someone close*. You never believe it'll ever happen to you. It was always the thing that happened to someone else, and you stood round feeling awkward, not knowing what to say; feeling sorrow for then, and hating the way they looked at you with their shocked, grief-dark eyes. Then one day it's your turn to look into the dead face of a close one, a loved one, and to remember the laughter, the smiles and frowns, the good and bad memories; and it's you who has the empty feeling, you who knows the reason for the empty stares and the clumsy words coming from numb lips.

Matthew rose stiffly to his feet. He looked across at Jubal. 'Go fetch a blanket,' he said gently.

Turning, Matthew saw Sid still sitting against the front wall. Anger and revulsion boiled up inside him.

'Couldn't you at least have got off

your butt and paid a little respect? In case you forgot, Ned was your brother.' Matthew's big hands were clenched tight at his sides as he spat out the words.

Sid tilted back his head. 'Ain't goin' to give us a minute, are you, Matt?'

'Meaning?'

'Meanin' I'm a little tired of you givin' all the orders all the time. I done had my fill.' Sid shoved to his feet and confronted Matthew. 'All right, so Ned stopped a slug. I'm sorry — '

'*Sorry!* By God, Sid, if it hadn't been for getting you off that coach, none of us would be stuck here. Hoby wouldn't be lyin' over there. Ned wouldn't be stretched out like he is.'

'Christ, Matt, you sound more like Pa every time you open your stupid mouth.'

Something snapped inside Matthew Reece. Without warning or hesitation he hauled off and drove a heavy fist to Sid's mouth. Sid made a garbled sound as he lurched backward, slamming into the log wall. He hung there, his body held rigid, blood trickling from the corners of his mouth. Then he abruptly kicked away from the wall, smashing shoulder first into his brother. Locked together they crashed hard against the table. Sid's weight bore down across Matthew, forcing him flat down on the tabletop. For long seconds they wrestled, each seeking a good hold on the other. A grunt of pain spewed from Sid's lips as Matthew rammed a hard knee up into his stomach. It broke Sid's hold long enough to enable Matthew to push up, away from the table. As his feet touched the floor, Matthew swung his fist into Sid's face again, and as Sid backed off, Matthew slammed in a couple of hard punches to the stomach.

Blaine felt Katy's hand on his arm. He shook his head. 'Don't say it. This is one time I don't interfere.'

Though he was hurt Sid fought back hard, driving in blow after blow to Matthew's face and body.

Jubal came back into the room. He

stood awkwardly watching, his brutish face creased with indecision and puzzlement, while his brothers turned themselves into bloody, gasping, clawing images of men.

Now Sid fell to his knees. Matthew drove his head back with a stabbing backhand. He reached out with one hand and caught hold of Sid's shirt, hauling him to his feet, and then raked a heavy fist across Sid's mouth. Again Sid banged up against the wall, and again Matthew stepped in fast, driving hard, crippling punches to Sid's stomach until Sid, unable to hold himself upright, slid to the floor, curling up, clutching his stomach.

Matthew stepped back then, his powerful chest heaving raggedly. His broad face was bruised and scraped, streaked with blood. He stood back a few feet from where Sid lay, breathing hard through his swollen lips.

'*Matt?*' Jubal said slowly.

Matthew swung his head round. He looked from the blanket Jubal held to Ned's laid-out body.

'Put the blanket over Ned,' he said.

Jubal moved slowly to obey, still puzzled by the behavior of his brothers.

'First time Sid and me ever fought,' Matthew said to no one in particular. He took a damp cloth Katy handed him and eased his aching face. 'We had words, mind. Sid was always inclined to be stubborn.'

Blaine said, 'I'm sorry about Ned, Reece.'

'Really?' There was a touch of bitter sarcasm in Matthew's voice.

'Listen, Reece,' Blaine bit back, 'no matter what's gone between us, Ned was still a human being, a man, and I meant what I said. You take it any way you want, friend, but just try and realize we're not all like Sid.'

Matthew glanced across at Katy, then to Chad Butler. He faced Blaine again and was about to speak. For some reason he changed his mind. Picking up his rifle he returned to the window. He gazed out at the seemingly empty land; knowing, though, that the Apaches were still out there. His face hurt like hell, and there was a raw, throbbing area round his ribs. *Damn Sid*, he thought savagely. Weren't they all in enough trouble over him without fighting among themselves? Matthew's hands clenched tight around his rifle.

God, if I'd known it was going to be like this, Sid could have gone to Yuma and rotted. Ned was dead, Hoby was near to dying. All for one man who didn't even have the decency to pay respect to a brother who'd died fighting for him. Christ, what in hell had happened to Sid? Matthew didn't know the answer to that. But whatever else, he knew now that nothing could be the same; he'd never be able to forget, or forgive Sid's actions. Matthew bit back a groan as the pain in his face swelled suddenly, jaggedly.

Katy said, 'Ed, we've got only enough water for another half day.'

'And there'll be no chance of getting any from the creek,' Blaine said.

They were in the kitchen. Katy was

preparing a rough meal of cold side meat between hunks of bread. A kettle of water was beginning to boil on the stove; to light the stove they'd had to break up one of the kitchen chairs.

Katy made a pot of coffee and began pouring it into tin mugs.

'Ed, how much longer can we hold them off?'

Blaine turned away from the window. 'Hard to say. We've been lucky up to now. I reckon the Apaches have lost more men than they anticipated. I think they expected us to be easy meat. Now they've lost face, and Apaches don't like to lose face. They're fanatically proud. They need that victory over us more than ever now. By now they've realized that rushing us is only going to cut down their force even more, so they're going to sit it out and wait for us to make the wrong moves. I know the Apache, and at this sort of fighting he's master.'

Katy handed him a mug of steaming black coffee. 'Sounds like a stalemate,' she said.

Blaine helped himself to a sandwich. 'Unless we get help.'

'Ham?'

'Uh-uh. If nothing's gone wrong for him, he should be well on his way to Fort Kane. If we can hold out for a couple more days, maybe ... ' His words trailed off.

Katy picked up a tray of coffee and sandwiches and smiled at Blaine.

'We'll hold out,' she said.

Blaine watched her go out of the kitchen, wishing he had her simple faith in the words of someone she trusted.

The dangers they had to face weren't all outside now. They had trouble right in the middle of their own camp which might prove even more deadly than the Apaches.

★   ★   ★

Sid Reece let himself down on to a chair beside the table. He had brushed aside Jubal's clumsy attempt to help and forced himself to walk upright to the chair, despite the gut-wrenching pains in his stomach. Sid wiped blood from his mouth and chin with the back of his hand. He wanted to double up and lie down until the pain went away. But he wasn't going to give Matt the pleasure or satisfaction of seeing him do that. Sid glanced furtively across to where Matthew crouched at the window. *Christ, if I had me a gun now*. He pressed a hand to his aching stomach, felt tears brim over at the corners of his eyes and run down his grimy, unshaven face.

He suddenly found himself remembering the way he'd felt back in the coach, long before they reached Butler's Station. Remembered how he'd been telling himself he'd soon be a free, unchained man. How Matt would have everything fixed. Sid gave a bitter inward chuckle. Matt had sure done that. He'd fixed things fine. *Too damn fine*, Sid thought.

He looked round as Katy came in with a tray of coffee and sandwiches. Just the sight of her made him feel much better. Sid let his hungry eyes rove freely over her body, feeding on her beauty, lingering where her breasts thrust firmly against the thin shirt. He watched her as she took coffee and food to Matthew and Chad, then to Jubal. Leaving the tray on the table Katy passed Sid, and on her way out she raised her eyes and returned his gaze.

In her calm, cold eyes Sid could see the hate she carried for him mirrored crystal clear. Then she was gone from his sight, into the rear of the cabin.

Sid reached for a mug of coffee. He swallowed a mouthful of the scalding black liquid, feeling it burn its way down his throat. It eased the pain in his stomach slightly.

Across the room Sid could see Jubal watching him. Jubal's face wore a worried, uncertain expression. As Sid raised his head to stare at him, Jubal averted his gaze and made a pathetic attempt to appear disinterested. Sid swung his head round, gazing out over Matthew's shoulder toward the far-reaching land and sky. So near to freedom, yet so far away too. It would be dark in a few hours, he saw. A good time to make his getaway? After debating the question, Sid decided against it. He had no horse. On foot he'd not get far. Also, the Apaches were all round the cabin, and good as he was, Sid knew he'd stand no chance of getting past a line of waiting, watching Apaches. It was just the sort of thing they were anticipating. *When then?* Dawn? When the fighting broke out? Sid shook his head angrily. He'd have to play along with the rest for a time. Until he saw a really good opening. *But don't leave it too long,* he warned. That kid . . . what was his name . . . Ham, might have found help and be heading back right now.

Sid drained his coffee. He rubbed his aching stomach and promised to repay Matthew for every bruise.

23

During the night the Apaches slipped unseen through the darkness and removed their dead.

And two hours before dawn Hoby Reece died. Quietly, without even regaining full consciousness, he died, and left the hard, angry world that had fathered him without making his mark. Only Katy Warner was beside him when he breathed his life out. Katy called Matthew Reece across, and the outlaw sat beside the couch until it was light.

The last of the water was used to make a much-needed brew of coffee. They all drank gratefully, thankful for something to take their minds off the strain of waiting and watching. They talked only when necessary, and went about their duties with slow reluctance.

Outside the sun rose and began to climb. It promised to be another hot day. Hot and still, without a breath of wind to relieve the oppressive, smothering heat.

To the waiting Apaches the day meant more hours of patient waiting, broken by periodic bursts of sniping gunfire at the cabin. It was sometimes a long wait, but nearly always successful. Sooner or later the whites would break. Sooner . . . or later . . .

* * *

'Christ, how much longer we goin' to wait like this?' Harvy Martin came up off his chair shouting, his face pale and shining with sweat. He was tense, jittery, and dangerously near to breaking down. 'Penned up here like a bunch of scared steers. It's damn stupid! All for a few stinkin' Apaches.'

Blaine blocked Martin's path. He could see the nervous tremble in Martin's jaw, the abnormal gleam in the wildly staring eyes.

'It's rough on us all, boy,' Blaine said.

He was desperately trying to find the right words to use, for he knew that the wrong thing said right now could set Martin really going. 'Boy, I know how you feel. I have a notion to bust wide open myself. But it wouldn't help any, apart from getting me killed maybe.'

Matt said, 'Blaine's right, boy, you heed him. Going off half-cocked is liable to put you on your back with a gutful of lead. You'd do best to sit down and get some rest. One way or another we'll be getting some action soon.'

Martin's outburst took most of the panic out of him. He sank back on to his chair and closed his eyes.

'Thanks, Reece,' Blaine said.

Matthew Reece shrugged it off. 'We need all the guns we got. Alive and firing.'

But somewhere at the back of his mind Blaine had an idea that Matthew Reece hadn't given him the real reason for calming down Harvy Martin.

Midday.

The heat bore down with sadistic persistence.

Shimmering waves of heat radiated across the open land, giving the far-distant horizon a trembling, almost live appearance.

Blaine perched himself on a chair and tried to ignore the cloying heat. It was a pointless endeavor. His every movement, even breathing, was the signal for a fresh outburst of sweating. His shirt and pants clung to him greasily. He felt dirty and unshaven. And tired. For the first time in long hours he became aware of his bandaged shoulder; aware of a seemingly distant throb, endurable and only noticed now because he wasn't concentrating on other matters.

But when he realized that, he did concentrate on other matters, on the problems that surrounded and dogged them. It helped him to forget his personal condition.

This was the third day, he calculated tiredly. Their ammunition was still in good supply. So too was food. But they had no more water. Getting it from the creek was out of the question. No matter how close it seemed to the cabin, no matter how the coolness of it sparkled in the sunlight, it might as well be a million miles away. Step outside with an empty bucket and start to walk across the deserted, silent ground. Then hear the silence rock with the jarring crash of hidden rifles; watch the bucket fly from nerveless fingers as heavy slugs rip into yielding flesh, shattering bones and vital organs. And the choking dust clogs mouth and nose while the cool creek-water flows by undisturbed . . . Blaine could imagine the scene with vivid clarity, a picture brought on by heat and exhaustion, and the dry thirst that was clawing at his throat.

Blaine rubbed his eyes, wiping the smarting beads of sweat from them. Raising his head, he met Sid Reece's hard stare from the other side of the room. Since the fight with Matthew, Sid had retreated into a sullen, silent mood. He said nothing, did nothing, but sat in a corner, brooding. Blaine could almost see the sneering smile Sid was inwardly enjoying. He felt his anger rising and checked it. It happened every time he came in contact with Sid, and he knew it must not get the better of him.

Sid was only waiting for a chance to start something. He would never be satisfied until he had settled with Blaine.

And that meant only one thing to Sid's way of thinking. To hurt and kill. Not for Sid Reece the subtle ways of attack; he was a simple man with a single-track mind; an easy man to figure. When Sid was hurt his one desire was to repay that hurt in kind. Eye for eye, tooth for tooth.

Just the opposite was Matthew Reece. Tough, ruthless, yet a man of feeling, who could assess and evaluate a situation so that he came out on the right side. But at the same time, Blaine had to admit, there were some things about Matthew Reece that were out of character. The way he was acting toward people who, only a short time ago, he was ready to kill, for instance. Were Matthew's actions genuine?

Or was he just adapting this outward appearance to fit the needs of the present situation? Blaine didn't know. But he had enough sense to realize that Matthew would need as much watching as Sid. That was enough for Blaine. He held that when a man tried to figure out what made another man tick, he was getting into something that went beyond the limits of flesh and blood and bone. There was enough on a man's outside to handle, without trying to pick his brains.

Toward dusk the Apaches opened fire again. It held until dark. During that time the cabin was raked on all sides by the heavy rifle fire. The walls were too thick for the slugs to penetrate. Another night brought silence again, and cold, and more of the inevitable waiting.

They moved the blanket-covered bodies into one of the back bedrooms.

Out beyond the corral a single small fire could be seen.

It lit up the night's blackness, winking throughout the long hours like a reminding beacon, and those in the cabin could almost hear its silent message: *We are here, still. And we shall stay until the time is right. We shall wait.*

24

It happened just before noon of the next day.

Since dawn the Apaches had kept up sporadic gunfire.

All morning their slugs had been hammering at the cabin walls, and occasionally one would come through a gap.

Then the firing ceased. It did not fade out gradually. It ceased completely, abruptly. Silence, so acute it was almost painful, descended.

And the occupants of the cabin looked at one another with questions frozen on their parched lips, wondering what would happen next. From the bullet-scarred window and door they could see the land spread out naked and empty.

Nothing was in sight; nothing moved.

'What the devil are they up to?' Chad Butler asked.

'We're getting the silent treatment

now,' Blaine told him. 'A touch of Apache craft. They've gotten us used to the sound of continuous gunfire. And then they take it away. Leave us in silence, leave us guessing as to why they've stopped shooting. Let it prey on our minds while we wonder if maybe they're moving in.'

'Maybe they are,' Chad said.

'Why should they? We can't get out. So they'll just squat outside and wait.'

'Maybe the bastards have pulled out,' Chad said dryly, a wry smile playing nervously round the corners of his cracked lips. He didn't think they had for one minute.

Over in the far corner Harvy Martin furtively raised his head from the floor where he'd been resting. The deputy's face was pale and lined, his eyes glassy and unblinking. His hands trembled as he reached for his rifle, sat up with his back to the wall.

Harvy Martin was scared. Of dying, of being caught alive by the Apaches. He wanted to be out and away from this place fast. Before it was too late. Like it had been too late for the others. He shivered violently as he recalled the way Ned Reece had died; he'd been right beside the outlaw when the heavy slug had struck. Martin saw the scene all over again every time he closed his eyes. He wasn't going to end up like that, with the back of his skull blown off and his brains splattered over a wall. He had to get out. Blaine had been wrong in making them stay. They should have taken the horses and gone fast. But no, Blaine had said stay and fight. And they had. The Apaches had run off the horses, blocked off their water and killed three of them.

Gone was all the smug self-assurance, the cocky arrogance. In its place was a scared kid. The shiny badge on his shirt didn't mean a thing to Martin now, as he sat trembling with fear. The rising tide of panic that had been quelled the day before began to take control again.

Stronger this time, feeding upon his fear and upsetting his judgment. By the time he got to his feet Harvy Martin was no longer master of his own will; it was controlled by panic, blind unreasoning panic, born of desperation and loss of nerve.

In the jumbled, fear-paralyzed chambers of his mind there was one clear thought that he could comprehend. Get out. Get away from the cabin and its stink, its filth and smell of death. It was clean outside and so peaceful, silent.

The Apaches were gone by now. *That's the real reason they stopped shooting. They've pulled out.*

Without being fully conscious of his actions, Martin headed for the door. So abrupt was his move, no one noticed him until he was tugging at furniture blocking the doorway.

'Hey, boy, where the hell do you think you're heading?'

Martin ignored Blaine's challenge, continued tugging at the furniture.

'*Martin!*' Blaine's voice was hard, commanding.

Chad Butler was closer to Martin.

He put a hand on the deputy's shoulder.

Martin's head snapped round. He stared at Chad without seeing him. And Chad recognized the look in Martin's eyes to be the mark of a sick man.

'Blaine, quick,' Chad yelled, and made a grab at Martin.

But the deputy was too fast. He slammed his rifle butt into Chad's stomach, then swung it up against Chad's jaw. Chad spun back, away from the door, colliding with Blaine.

It was all the time Martin needed to step outside into the searing open glare of the station-yard. He hesitated for a moment, then headed out past the empty corral.

Someone was shouting from the cabin. Martin heard, but the sound didn't register. He was too involved in his attempt at escape to be distracted by insignificant voices.

Then the voice faded away as he crested a short ridge and went down the opposite side, leaving the cabin out of sight behind him.

Here, the silence and emptiness of the land seemed limitless. It spread far and wide in every direction; vast and breathtaking in its savage magnificence.

Harvy Martin paused to wipe his sweating face. His mind raced wildly in tortured confusion. *Calm down*, he told himself. *You won't get far if you don't hold it down and do some figuring.* He glanced round the featureless landscape with a weary sigh. *Christ, it all looks the same.*

Which way to safety? Which to death? Wait, though. The Butler kid, Ham, he headed north-west. Martin nodded in decisive haste. Northwest it was. With any luck he might even meet up with the patrol the kid went looking for. If the kid had got through, that was. Even so, it was going to be a long hot walk. Hell, he could join up with the creek a few miles upstream and get some water. If only he'd brought a canteen along. Couldn't think of everything at a time like this.

At least you're alive, boy. And that is something. Let those fools sit and rot in that cabin, waiting for the Apaches who weren't coming.

Martin gave a dry, jerky chuckle out loud. He turned and began his long walk. He took four steps and stopped dead in midstride, his laughter trailing off into a whimper of pure terror.

Standing in his path, no more than ten feet away, was a half-naked, painted Apache brave. A second Apache appeared on Martin's left. Then one on the right. And behind him the merest whisper of shifting sand told him there were others at his back.

He could feel the merciless stare of the unblinking black eyes, seething hatred mirrored there, could see the stone-hard faces, impassive and cold. All the stories he'd heard of Apache savagery came flooding back in a stomach-twisting coil of fear as the image of those primitive faces filled his eyes and mind like phantom shadows from a nightmare.

And in that moment of black despair

all sanity left him.

'*No!*' The sound he uttered burst from him like the cry of the damned. He lunged forward, too late to do anything but swing his rifle like a club at the nearest Apache face. But the face was gone before the slashing gun reached it. Martin staggered drunkenly, fell to his knees. Before he could recover his balance they were on him. His rifle was torn out of his hands. And then they began to beat him with their own weapons.

One of the Apaches rapped out a command and the beating stopped. Martin was dragged to his feet and forced to walk, following the one who had spoken, and who was obviously the leader of the group. They angled away from the station, and finally came to a place where a bunch of sturdy ponies stood tethered. The ground nearby was dotted with Apache gear and black ash circles showed where they'd had their fires. To one side lay blanket-covered shapes and even Harvy Martin was able to recognize them as the Apache dead. And a sudden thought leapt wildly up at him: What were the Apaches going to do to him? With all those braves dead they weren't going to feel in sympathy with a white man who had helped to kill their comrades. And once more the thought of escape came to him.

He had no more time to do anything but think about it.

The Apache leader said something to his warriors. Their reaction was to seize Martin and strip him naked, then draw him to the ground. Rawhide thongs were produced and tied around his ankles and wrists, then the thongs were fastened to short wooden stakes hammered into the ground, spread-eagling him to the hot earth.

Martin needed no telling. Even in his half-crazed, panic jumbled state he knew what was going to happen; and to him came the mocking realization that it was this very thing he'd been trying to run away from. And he did what to him was the only thing to do. He kicked and jerked at the rawhide thongs until his flesh tore and his hands and feet were red with his own blood. He tried but failed to prevent his bladder from emptying itself.

And the Apaches stood and watched him and waited until he had exhausted himself. They were masters at this form of torture, and knew what took place with each new victim.

Again the Apache leader spoke. One word; a flat, hard sound against the hot air.

Through fear-misted eyes Martin saw one of the braves move in and squat beside him. The Apache held a slim-bladed knife in one brown hand. The sunlight danced along the keen edge and made a many-pointed star on the needle point.

'*Oh, God, no. Please. No!*' Martin screamed.

And the Apaches smiled to one another. This one would make much noise as his white body flipped and rolled in the agony that would follow.

Unleashed, the words poured from Martin's dribbling mouth, tumbling wildly, jerkily, one over the other.

Begging, pleading, crying words that fell on alien ears.

The star on the tip of the knife winked at him, then vanished as the Apache lowered the blade. Martin felt the pin-prick against his stomach and his whole body shuddered with uncontrollable violence. Ice-cold fear wrenched at his insides. He could feel the knife being stroked back and forth over his stomach. Then there was a swift slicing motion and the blade cleaved the flesh, leaving a long, pink-lined, blood-dribbling gash.

A line of burning heat lanced across Martin's stomach.

His body quivered, arched upwards from the ground in protest against the pain. He could feel blood running hotly down his groin.

He began to scream after the third sweep of the knife.

★　★　★

250

They sat and listened to Harvy Martin's screams for three hours. And when they stopped the tension grew even heavier.

'At least we knew he was still alive,' Chad Butler said. His jaw was covered by a large bruise beneath his thick stubble and it was making it hard to talk.

'Maybe he . . . he's dead,' Katy said. 'If he is, we should be thankful.'

'For what? So you don't have to listen to him scream?' Tom Peak snapped at her.

'Thankful that's he's no longer in pain, Mr. Peak. You were his friend. I would have understood.'

Peak rubbed his face and gave a tired sigh. 'Sorry, ma'am, didn't mean to be sharp. I'm not feeling up to it just now.'

'Are any of us?' Katy asked.

It was an hour later when Jubal Reece called them over to the window.

Coming across the station-yard was a slow-walking Apache pony. Yards from the cabin the pony halted and pawed at the dusty ground.

On the pony's back sat a figure that might have been Apache or white. It was tied to the pony to prevent it from falling, with a cross of wood supporting the back, for it was in no state to support itself. Once it had been a man. Young and whole and healthy. And then it had a name . . . Harvy Martin.

But now it was a pitiful thing that only remotely resembled a man in its basic shape. The body was reduced to a raw hunk of butchered meat. The hands and feet had been burned off. All that remained were blackened stumps. The face was featureless. Only the eyes were untouched and they gazed out from the destroyed face in mute terror. From the bleeding gash of the mouth rolled a low bubbling moan of sheer animal hurt. The tongue had been cut out. The sound came from an injured creature asking for swift relief from hellish pain so that it could rest in peace.

'*Sonofabitch.*' The word burst sharp and clear on the empty silence that lay over the room. And Blaine was surprised when he realized the word was his own.

'Keep away, Katy,' Chad said. He turned from the window and pulled her into the room before she could see outside. His face was pale and there was a sick look in his eyes.

'You want to do it?' Matthew Reece asked quietly, suddenly.

Blaine glanced at him and saw the .45 Matthew was holding. He glanced outside. The pony had moved away from the cabin a little. Martin's head lolled slackly on his bloody chest and bright blood ran freely from his mouth and nose.

'No chance?' Blaine asked. He was hoping against hope. But he knew the answer before Matthew spoke; he'd seen too many men like this, after the Apache knives had done their work, and he'd seen most of those men die. Those that didn't, lived out their lives as chair-ridden cripples.

'Would you want to live in that

condition? Anyhow, he won't because they've hurt him bad. He's bleeding from deep inside. It's just a matter of how long it takes him to bleed to death.'

Blaine took the Colt. He thumbed back the hammer.

Matthew drew away from the window and left him alone.

'God forgive me,' Blaine said softly. 'I'm sorry, boy.' He raised the Colt, aimed and fired twice. Both slugs took Martin in the head. Blood spurted and dappled the pony's flanks. The animal whinnied nervously and backed off, then turned and cantered back the way it had come.

Blaine dropped the smoking gun. He was trembling.

His stomach churned violently. Then he leaned his head and shoulders out of the window and was sick.

25

They waited out the day in silent expectation. Hoping for a miracle, but not really expecting one.

To Blaine, the soldier, this sort of situation was part of the job, his life, his calling, though he never thought of himself as the dedicated kind. But this time there was a difference. This time there wasn't just the threat of the enemy outside. This time there was an enemy inside, fighting alongside him, and maybe planning Blaine's death at the same time. Blaine was fighting on two levels: the direct and open hostilities of the attacking Apaches; and at the same time he was constantly on the watch for a move from the enemy at his side, wondering how and when and where it would come. Because he knew it *would* come.

Sometime it would come. It was just a matter of who got to him first, the

Apaches or this enemy inside.

And there was Katy too. Once he had lost her; but now she was beside him again, and he was not going to take the chance of losing her again. He reflected then that fate had dealt him a pretty mixed hand. He had gained and lost.

But he reckoned that what he had gained made up for the losses. Given a fair shake, he might still come out with a full hand. A winning hand.

Katy Warner, the young woman who had tried to run from life, and now found herself face to face with death. But she was content because she was with her man and she wanted nothing more from life. She was satisfied to be with him, to stay, to follow him. Be it life or death, she was beside him; and that was how it was, and she was content.

There was the station-manager, waiting for one thing. The return of his son. A man who had found his peace with the world in the light of his boy's attaining manhood. The years of work and thought that had finally paid off in the only way it could. Chad Butler was no great man, just one among many in this great sprawling land. But he had made his mark, no matter how small, and he was justly proud. And for him, life was something worth fighting for.

And the lawman, Tom Peak. He had seen his two companions die. One had gone quick and clean; if any form of dying could be labeled quick or clean. The other had gone the hard way. The way no man should die, screaming in pain and terror, his body reduced to an obscene mass of tortured flesh.

Peak waited out his time in bitter silence. He was a man used to violence and sudden death. But the way the lives of McAllister and Martin had been taken left him sick and angry. He could name the cause . . . Sid Reece. He held him totally responsible. Sid Reece's being freed from the coach had resulted in Marshal McAllister's death. Cause and effect had brought down the Apaches on them. And Harvy Martin, young and inexperienced, had been unable to take it. He had panicked. And died. Nor did Peak forget Sam Loren, the stage driver, or the guard, Will Hakin. Four good men dead so that one man could walk free, a man not fit to clean their boots. It was a poor exchange; four had died so that one could live. The long years of keeping law and order, of following the book, were lost in the unreasoning flood of blind anger that enveloped him. Tom Peak made a vow to himself that Sid Reece would not go without paying for what he had done. Peak swore he would see to it. Even if he had to kill Sid himself.

Sid Reece had seen what the Apaches had done to Harvy Martin. He had derived a certain amount of satisfaction from it. Damn if it didn't save him the trouble of settling with the bastard himself. Now, Sid squatted on his heels against the wall and chuckled softly to himself. At the same time as he got himself killed, Sid thought, the dumb kid had shown Sid here that trying to sneak out was no-go. Worry gnawed at Sid's insides though. Things were getting close now. Too close. No use pretending. Things were pretty grim. Getting out of this alive was going to be damn tricky. It would take all of a man's cunning and craft. But he was going to have a damn good try. The hell with the rest of them. They were capable of looking after themselves. If they weren't, they'd end up like Ned or Hoby or Martin. But not old Sid. No sir, this mother's son was in no mind for that kind of end.

He switched his attention to the woman. No matter what, he decided, it was worth the risk to have her. When he left here, he intended her to be with him. He'd probably have to gun Blaine. That was no problem. Blaine was a soldier, not a gunfighter. And it would be worth facing a dozen Blaines for that flame-haired beauty. Up in the snow-country where Sid planned going, a woman like her could make lonely days and nights something other than lonesome. Sid grinned again. Nights got real cold up there. But with her along, a problem like that was easily solved. He had no doubts as to the fact that she would fight him every inch of the way. But even the hardest-headed broncs could be busted in time. And if things worked out the way Sid was hoping they would, time was something they would have plenty of.

Matthew Reece was wondering how much time they had left. Because it was getting to the stage where time was all they did have left. There was nothing else. Unless the Butler boy brought help. *Then what?* Maybe the Apaches would be beaten off. And then the army would step in and take him. Matthew had no expectations of an easy way out. Either way, Apaches or army, it would be the way of the gun. He was no fool. The odds were against him. He could end it now. Go outside and take as many of the Apaches with him as he could. But that was not Matthew

Reece's way. For despite the certain knowledge that his trail was coming to a blind canyon, there was at the back of his mind a faint glimmer of hope that always showed itself to him in moments like these, and told him to hang on. Don't give in until the last possible moment. Keep your freedom as long as you can because it is something worth keeping. A man without his freedom might as well be dead. And it didn't end with himself. There was Jubal to look out for. Big, slow, clumsy Jubal. A giant in body, but a child in his thinking and outlook. Having to be led, to be told what to do. To have everything explained carefully before being able to grasp its meaning. Jubal, so physically strong, yet in effect the weakest of them all.

Matthew found himself thinking of Sid; but bitterness was strong inside him, and he pushed the dark thoughts aside and tried to forget.

★ ★ ★

The Apache squatted motionless in the dust. He had a blanket draped over his head and back to keep off the hot sun.

His warriors were spread out around the cabin. Waiting and watching.

Chana was angry. Things had not gone well. They had not yet destroyed the whites in Butler's Station. He wished he could speak the tongue of the whites; then he could have questioned the one they had tortured. But the white had only screamed and sobbed as his body tossed and jerked beneath the knives of his captors.

It had given much pleasure to see the white's agonized struggles and to hear him scream. Chana had hoped the spirit of Torrio could hear. This would ease its restlessness.

This much Chana had been able to do for his dead friend.

But it was not enough. On the memory of his father Chana had sworn to kill all the *Pinda Lickoyi* at the station. This he would do.

This he must do. He could not fail.

Failure was not possible. Failure was not permissible.

Chana threw off his blanket and rose to his full height.

'*Aaaiiieee!*'

Sweeping across the open land his shrill cry cut the silent air with the sting of a whiplash.

The time of waiting was over.

The time of vengeance had come.

Heads snapped up. Eyes widened with alarm and bodies became tense and rigid.

★　★　★

The violence of the screeching yell broke the drowsy lull that had settled over the cabin.

They came alert as one. Weapons ready, they took up their pre-appointed positions. Each knew somehow that the time had come. It was now that their fate would be settled, decided.

Each wondered about the outcome.

Victory or defeat?

Live or die?
Who could tell? Who could know?
Quien sabe?

26

The Apaches hit the cabin hard and fast. They came out of the desert and the brush, running in erratic curves, bobbing and weaving, their weapons sending a deadly stream of lead slugs and flint-tipped arrows.

Out of the original band there were now only eleven; eleven vengeful warriors intent on only one thing. To kill every white in the cabin. Gone now was the craft, the caution that had made them wait. That was over. In its place was raw fighting fury, the driving blood-lust that could carry a man clear through hell and back.

And not even the roar of the guns could drown the searing howls and screeches of the Apaches as they made their last run at the cabin.

★ ★ ★

'Make every shot count. We might not get another chance,' Blaine yelled above the rolling drum of rifle fire.

He was back at the barricaded door. Katy was beside him, a Henry repeater in her hands. At the front window were Matthew Reece and Chad Butler. Sid and Jubal Reece, along with Tom Peak were in the back of the cabin.

The sound of the guns was deafening, and the hot air was thick with the stench of burned powder.

Blaine saw this attack as the decider in this lonely fight.

This time it would be won or lost.

He snapped off a shot at a leaping figure by the corral.

And missed. The Apache paused to aim his own weapon.

Blaine fired again. This time it was not a miss. The Apache dropped his rifle and clutched at the red patch on his chest; then he fell on to his face and did not move again.

Katy loosed off shot after shot with methodical coolness. And she downed two bucks. One got up again and came on, dragging his left leg in the dust, but the second one stayed down, with Katy's slug lodged deep inside his skull.

Slowly the Apaches drove the defenders from their positions. Reluctantly the whites were forced to leave the front of the cabin and find what cover they could behind the room's furniture.

Then an Apache threw himself headlong through the window. He hit the floor lightly, rolled and came to his feet with his rifle swinging up.

Matthew and Chad and Blaine fired as one. The Apache was slammed back against the wall with sickening force. He hung there for a moment, then toppled on to his face.

A second Apache appeared at the window and two came through the door.

'Ed, the door,' Katy yelled.

She swung her rifle round and let go a shot. The slug hit the Apache in the right eye and came out the back of his head. Blood and bits of flesh spattered the face of the buck behind him.

The shaft the Apache had been about to loose jerked off-target. Then the buck let it go. It lanced cross the room and took Chad Butler in the left arm, pinning him to the log wall.

Before the buck could notch a second shaft Blaine drove a shot at him. The Apache gave a harsh scream as the slug ripped open his throat in a flash of red.

Turning to Chad, Blaine yanked the shaft free with a savage jerk. Chad slumped to the floor with a low moan.

Blaine stripped off Chad's belt and strapped it tight around the arm above the wound. He hoped it would help stop the blood that was gushing from the ragged hole.

A thrashing figure fell through the curtains that led into the rear of the cabin. It was Jubal Reece. A long Apache lance was buried deep in his chest. The big man was screaming like a hurt child. A high, shrill sound that hammered at the ears and made stomachs tighten.

Then Sid Reece backed through the curtains. Close after him was Tom Peak.

'They were too fast for us,' Peak shouted. His gun was empty and he threw it aside.

Like something out of a madman's nightmare the cabin became the scene of a savage slaughter. The Apaches came in like avenging demons. Rifles were no good in this kind of situation; they were reversed and used as clubs. It became a hand-to-hand fight, a desperate kill-or-be-killed struggle. It was crude and brutal, cold and utterly devoid of mercy. Red man fought white in frantic, close-quarter combat.

Blaine found himself struggling with a near-naked buck who seemed intent on burying his knife in Blaine's throat.

He very nearly succeeded. But then Blaine remembered the lessons he'd been taught about this kind of fighting.

Lessons taught to him by the tough masters of a rough school. They had been soldiers, like him, but they had been in uniform a lot longer. And what they didn't know about frontier fighting wasn't worth the trouble of finding out. Blaine remembered those lessons and put the knowledge to good use.

The Apache gave an agonized scream as Blaine's knee slammed upwards, ripping into his groin. Taking swift advantage of his opponent's relaxation, Blaine used both hands to twist the Apache's knife so that it faced its owner. Blaine shoved, hard, and the knife sliced into the Apache's stomach. The Apache fell to his knees. Blaine yanked the knife free as the Apache fell away, leaning in to deliver killing slash to the Apache's throat.

Blaine turned, searching for Katy. Someone slammed into him, crashing him against the wall. He saw a sweating, hate-filled face looming out of the mist that fogged his eyes. Strong hands clamped around his throat and he felt his breath being cut off. There was a roaring in his ears, and his heart pounded wildly. Blaine clawed at the hands around his throat, but his fingers slipped on the greasy dark skin.

Far off it seemed he could hear the noise of the conflict. It rose and fell in volume. Blaine strained to see through the pulsing redness that swam before his eyes.

Searing heat circled his lungs and he began to cough harshly.

Blindly he lashed out with clenched fists. They struck something solid and he heard a pained grunt from his attacker. His clawing fingers found the man's hair, and Blaine hung on. He yanked hard, pulling back the man's head, heard the sharp intake of breath as he applied more pressure. But the fingers clamped tight around his throat didn't slacken. Blaine felt himself weakening. He knew he couldn't hold out much longer.

Chana, for it was he who had chosen Blaine, closed his fingers even tighter. In the frantic clash of men inside the cabin he had lost his weapons. And he had seen the swift brutal way that Blaine had dispatched one of his warriors.

In a blinding surge of passionate anger and hate the Apache had hurled himself at the *Pinda Lickoyi*. With the white momentarily stunned, it had been easy to get him by the throat.

If Chana had been expecting an easy victory over the white, he was swiftly disillusioned. The clawing hands of the white had snatched at Chana's hair and jerked his head back savagely. Chana could feel the muscles in his neck popping as the white put on more pressure. His head was bent far back, and he was finding it hard to breathe.

Would the *Pinda Lickoyi* not die? Or would Chana die first? For surely his neck would snap like a rotten twig soon if it was not released. The Apache gave a grunt of anger and pain.

He must kill the white. Too many of the Apache had died in this fight. The final victory must go to the Apache.

And then, above the roaring throb of blood that filled his ears, Chana heard a loud crashing explosion. He felt a tremendous blow just below his left shoulder blade. A line of fire lanced straight to his heart, and a spreading weakness began to engulf him. It spread along his arms until it washed out along his hands. Chana knew then that he had been shot. He made an effort to retain his hold on the white, but his fingers no longer obeyed him. They slid from the white's throat. Chana's arms fell to his sides, limp and heavy. Unable to stop himself, Chana fell to the floor. He lay on his stomach, his face pressed against the rough floorboards. He lifted his head; it had become very heavy, too, and looked about the room. He saw a white leaning against the wall. The white held a hand to his left arm and Chana saw blood on the sleeve of his shirt and on the man's fingers.

A second white sat against the same wall. He wore a silver badge pinned to the front of his filthy, bloodied shirt.

Movement on his left. And Chana saw another white move into view. This was a big man, with a broad hard face. He held a long-barreled revolving pistol in one big hand, and a faint curl of smoke came from the black muzzle.

There were others too. But Chana looked no further.

Not one of his warriors stood. Like himself they lay at the feet of the *Pinda Lickoyi*. Dead. Destroyed by the very ones they had hoped to destroy. Chana realized defeat for the first time in his life. If this was to be the way of it, the Apache would soon be wiped out. The whites here had fought well. Too well for the Apache. But there was no pride in defeat. Nor did Chana feel any. Only shame at his failure, and sorrow for his people, who, he saw now, would soon be crushed forever.

Chana lay his head down. By raising his eyes he could see through the window to the wide, clear sky beyond. A great sadness came over him as he thought of his beautiful land. So vast and high and empty. So free and untouched. But soon the *Pinda Lickoyi* would come in their thousands and build their towns and plant their fences and take the land.

Maybe, then, it was better that the Apache died, so that his people would not see the desecration of their beloved lands.

'*Death, take this weary child, for he tires of this world . . .* '

The chanted words bubbled through bloodied lips. As darkness began to fall over the land outside, Chana closed his eyes and gave himself to the waiting arms of Death.

★   ★   ★

'Thought you weren't going to make it there, Blaine.'

The mist was gone from his eyes, and Blaine saw it was Tom Peak who spoke.

'Likewise,' Blaine said. His voice came out a rattling croak. His throat felt swollen, and it hurt with every breath.

Katy dropped to her knees beside him, a mug of clear water in her hand. He drank, felt the soothing coolness of the water. He stared at the empty mug, and then the realization hit him. Fresh water from the creek.

'The Apaches?'

'Dead. All of them,' Matthew Reece told him flatly.

'We whipped 'em. Every last mother's son,' Chad crowed, clutching his wounded arm.

'My God. I never would have bet on it,' Blaine said softly.

And he was speaking for them all.

The dead Apaches were carried outside, and Jubal Reece was laid out beside his brothers.

The Apache ponies were brought in and turned into the corral.

Katy cleaned up the wounds and bound them up as best she could with her dwindling supply of medicinals. Then she got a fire going and boiled up coffee that was drunk by the mugful.

By midnight they were able to pause and eat.

Antagonism and hatred, the fear of one another was forgotten as exhaustion came upon them. They were for the moment content that they still lived. They carried their weapons, but made no move to use them. Enemies before, they had been brought together for a time by a common threat that could have destroyed them all. Now they were tired and sick of killing, even Sid Reece. They needed rest. Though each knew that with the dawn matters would have to be settled.

They found places to bed down around the room, placing their backs to the stout walls. Each tried to stay awake, but one by one they surrendered to sleep.

Blaine fought it off for a while. But he too finally gave up. Beside him, Katy slept deeply, silently. He saw her face in the soft light from the fire, and he found comfort in it. He relaxed, no longer fighting the leaden mantle of sleep.

The darkness became denser, then engulfed him completely, and he knew no more.

27

Blaine came awake with a jerk. It was well after dawn. Sunlight burst before his opened eyes, and he blinked them clear. And something was wrong. He looked round the room. The others still slept. Matthew Reece. Chad Butler. Tom Peak.

Sid . . . Where was Sid?

Then he saw the open door. And heard at that moment the sound of a woman's cry. It lasted for long seconds, then ceased abruptly.

He twisted round. Katy's blanket was empty.

Katy.

Sid Reece.

Blaine shoved to his feet. He yanked the Colt from his belt and headed for the door. Ignoring the pulsing ache from his shoulder. Stepped outside. And froze.

The corral gate was open, and Sid

already had two ponies roped. Katy was on one of them. Sid had a gun on her, as he draped a pair of filled saddlebags and two canteens across his own pony.

Blaine stepped clear of the cabin, halted midway to the corral.

'Reece, hold it. You're not going *anywhere*.'

Sid moved fast. His gun never wavered from Katy. He gathered up both ropes and walked the ponies from the corral. He halted them ten feet from Blaine.

'You're wrong, soldier. I am going somewhere.' Sid waggled the gun. 'The lady is going with me. And I don't think you're going to stop me.'

Blaine thumbed back the Colt's hammer. He didn't look at Katy.

'Go ahead,' Sid said. 'Only remember that I can drop her before I go.'

'That won't help you any,' Blaine snapped. He was getting worried because he knew Sid to be the sort who would do it without hesitation.

'Soldier, get out of my way. Or are you anxious to see the lady get her head blown off?' Sid was getting angry, confused, and it showed in his voice.

Blaine chanced a look at Katy. She sat her pony in silence, knowing enough to stay quiet.

'You movin', soldier?' Sid repeated. 'You ain't goin' to stop me.'

'He might not, Sid, but *I* will.'

Sid's head snapped round.

Matthew Reece stepped into view, just ahead of Blaine and to his right.

'Well, brother, at least I get a chance to say goodbye,' Sid said. He grinned. 'But don't you try to make me stay either.'

'Sid, if you don't put the gun down, I'll stop you. Permanently.'

Matthew's fingers brushed the butt of his tied-down gun.

Sid's eyes flicked from his brother to Blaine and back to Matthew.

'Why couldn't you just leave things lay, Matt? Damn you,' he screamed then. 'You just never learned when to let up.'

As he spoke, Sid swung his gun

round to line up on Matthew.

Blaine yelled, 'Katy, get down!'

She slid off the pony and dropped flat to the ground.

Sid fired twice.

Blaine saw Matthew twist sideways and fall.

From the cabin a shotgun boomed. The charge hit Sid's pony. The animal staggered, screaming shrilly. Sid threw himself clear as the pony dropped.

Blaine bellied down on the ground, his gun cocked and ready. A haze of dust blew across his face. As it cleared he saw Sid, on his feet, heading for the corral. Sid was cursing loudly as he ran.

As Sid reached the corral he turned and triggered a frantic shot at Blaine. The slug kicked up a geyser of dirt in Blaine's face.

Blaine's gun rose and centered. He fired as Sid loosed a second shot.

The outlaw's slug clipped Blaine's sleeve.

Then Sid was spun around as

Blaine's slug hammered him in the chest. He swung an arm around one of the corral posts and held himself up, still cursing, to fire again.

Blaine shot him again.

The muzzle of Sid's gun sagged toward the ground. A great shudder coursed through his body as a patch of red began to spread across his dirty shirt directly over his heart. Sid raised his head as Blaine got up. Sid's mouth moved violently but no sound came out. Blood began to dribble from his lips. Reluctantly Sid began to slide down the corral post. He curled up in the dust at the base of the post. His head hit the dirt with a soft thud. Only his left foot moved, twitching gently for a while.

Blaine helped Katy to her feet.

'You all right?'

She nodded. 'Just confused. It all happened so fast. I was half-asleep when he made me go in the kitchen and get some supplies. I only came fully awake when he put me on the horse.

282

That's when I screamed and then . . . '

'Don't talk now. And don't worry. It's over,' Blaine told her.

Katy uttered a great sigh.

Blaine left her and crossed over to where Matthew Reece lay. He knelt beside the outlaw. He saw the two holes in Matthew's chest that slowly pumped out bright fresh blood, and knew there was nothing he could do.

Matthew stared at him for a moment. Then asked, 'Sid?'

'He's dead,' Blaine said. 'I'm sorry, Reece.'

'Don't be,' Matthew said bitterly. 'It was bound to happen sometime or other. Sid's been heading that way for a long time.'

'I reckon I ought to say thanks. It's the second time you've pulled me out of trouble.'

Matthew closed his eyes for a while.

'Why'd you do it?' Blaine asked.

Matthew laughed softly. 'Why? God knows. I don't. Maybe I decided to convert. Does a man have to have a reason?'

'Reece, a couple of days back you were ready to gun me down without giving me a chance. Today you stand by me against your own brother. At least tell me the reason I'm worth siding for.'

'When men go through what we have, it does something to them. It makes a difference. Maybe I spent too much time watching you practice what you preach. What you said about wanting to build a new land and to be part of it. Maybe it was something I've wanted to be part of all my life. Perhaps I didn't know it, but I somehow reckon I've spent most of my life going about it the wrong way. I ain't making excuses. Maybe I ain't even making sense.' He coughed, then spat blood. 'Or maybe I just didn't want to get thrown in some stinking jail for the rest of my life. This way is quicker. Cleaner. You savvy?'

Blaine nodded. 'Reckon I do.'

'You're a man to ride the river with, Blaine. Pity we didn't meet up before.

We could have done things, you and me.'

A spasm of pain shook his body. He drew in a great breath and fought to hold on to the life that was slowly draining away. Matthew Reece died as he had lived. Fighting, without asking for, or taking help. One of the tough breed, the lonely breed, who, if they were nothing else, were men.

'Ed, he could have been something better. Why did he choose such a life?' Katy asked.

Blaine got to his feet. 'Who knows what makes a man do the things he does? *Quien sabe*, honey?'

'I don't think I'll ever forget him,' she said softly.

Tom Peak came out of the cabin. He carried his shotgun over one arm. He wore a grim look on his face as he strode across to where Sid Reece lay.

Chad followed Peak outside. He stood over Matthew Reece for a moment. Then he glanced at Blaine. 'I won't ask questions, but I damn sure would like to know what made him tick.'

Blaine didn't answer. He was watching a cloud of dust sweeping in from the north-west. For a moment he wasn't sure. And then his doubts were swept away by the brassy call of a bugle.

'Looks like your boy made it, Chad,' he grinned, despite his aching body and his filthy clothes. He unconsciously rubbed the thick stubble on his grimy face.

Chad followed Blaine's arm. '*Hey*. Ham made it. My boy made it. I knew he would.'

He let out a wild whoop and started forward to meet the oncoming troop of cavalry from Fort Kane. And his son, Ham.

Tom Peak passed them on his way out. 'A little late, but still a welcome sight,' he said.

'You want to go out and meet them?' Katy said.

Blaine put his arms around her, kissed her, forgetting about his filthy state and his sore shoulder. 'No. Do you?'

Katy shook her head, saying, 'Why should I? I've got all the cavalry I need right here.'

Blaine didn't need to have that explained. He knew what it meant. It was all he needed to know.

And that was the way it should be.

Iron Eyes is pursuing ruthless outlaws Joe Hyams and Buster Jones. But the pair get the drop on him, and leave him for dead in the dust . . . Meanwhile, another man is on the bounty hunter's trail — gunfighter Wolfe, sworn to take his revenge on the man who left him missing one arm. Kidnapping Squirrel Sally, the woman besotted with Iron Eyes, Wolfe sets off across the prairie — intending to use her as bait to draw out his enemy . . .

THE DEVIL'S ANVIL

Steve Hayes

Two kill-crazy McClory cousins have busted out of Yuma Pen, heading for Indian Territory. Somebody has to bring them in — and the job falls to Deputy US Marshal Liberty Mercer, who sets off to run the outlaws to ground. But to reach the McCrory stronghold in Silver Rock Canyon, Mercer and her makeshift posse — Raven Bjorkman, her old friend; Latham Rawlins, brother of Liberty's one-time love Latigo; and the crooked Dunn brothers — must cross the deadly, searing desert known as the Devil's Anvil . . .